2-50
3

SOR

Sorrow of the Snows

Upendra Nath Ashk

Translated from the Hindi by
Jai Ratan

HARPER PERENNIAL

NEW YORK · LONDON · TORONTO · SYDNEY · NEW DELHI · AUCKLAND

HARPER ● PERENNIAL

Published in India in 2011 by Harper
An imprint of HarperCollins *Publishers* India
A joint venture with
The India Today Group

First published in India as *Sorrow of the Snows* in 1971 by the Writers Workshop, Calcutta

ISBN: 978-93-5029-117-7

2 4 6 8 10 9 7 5 3 1

Upendra Nath Ashk asserts the moral right to be identified
as the author of this book.

This is a work of fiction and all characters and incidents described in this book are the
product of the author's imagination. Any resemblance to actual persons, living or dead, is
entirely coincidental.

HarperCollins *Publishers*
A-53, Sector 57, NOIDA, Uttar Pradesh – 201301, India
77-85 Fulham Palace Road, London W6 8JB, United Kingdom
Hazelton Lanes, 55 Avenue Road, Suite 2900, Toronto, Ontario M5R 3L2
and 1995 Markham Road, Scarborough, Ontario M1B 5M8, Canada
25 Ryde Road, Pymble, Sydney, NSW 2073, Australia
31 View Road, Glenfield, Auckland 10, New Zealand
10 East 53rd Street, New York NY 10022, USA

Typeset in 11/14.8 Arno Pro
Jojy Philip New Delhi 110 015

Printed and bound at
Thomson Press (India) Ltd.

For Khushwant Singh,
in memory of the time spent with him
in Kasauli

ONE

Dawn had not yet broken when the cock crowed a second time disturbing Hasandin in his sleep. He opened his eyes, but made no sign of getting up. He lay still for a long time, waiting for another rooster to take up the call or a dog to bark or a door to creak. When no sound came from anywhere, Hasandin realized that it was still some time for the morning to come. He pulled up the blanket over his body and tried to nap a little more. He had not been able to solicit any business for the past two days and this disturbed his mind, chasing away sleep. At last, when the cock gave a full-throated and lusty call again coaxing the villagers to get up, Hasandin threw away his blanket. As he took out the extinguished *kangri* from under his *firan,* he suddenly remembered how as a child he had burnt his *firan* with the *kangri* and had received a severe thrashing for his carelessness.

What a boon this *kangri* is! Hasandin thought. How would the people of Kashmir live without it? … Whether boatman or peasant, shepherd or *pandit,* they were all steeped in poverty. It was only on festive occasions such as *Eid* or *Navratra* that they could have a *firan* stitched and that too only once in several years. They wore it all the time—day or night, winter or summer. Could there be a greater calamity than to have one's *firan* burnt? It was right for his father to have thrashed him. For that matter he had bullied his own child into learning the use of the *kangri!*

With groping hands, he carefully put away the *kangri* in a corner, took the blanket, coiled it around his neck and got up. He looked at his sleeping wife and child in the darkness and then crossing the heap of grass lying to his left, he walked over to the window with measured steps. Removing the wooden bar, he peered into the darkness trying to guess the time.

It was not yet dawn, but the darkness outside had already faded to grey. Through the haze, one could see the overcast sky. The cock crowed again and from the other end of the village another rooster, younger in age—you could tell from its full-throated high-pitched voice—took up the challenge. A dog, which had been sleeping in the warmth of the stable below, came out and, raising his head to the sky, howled as if accusing those roosters of disturbing his sleep and asking God to destroy those wretched chanters with His divine wrath.

Hasandin closed the window without bolting it. A thin ray of grey light coming through the aperture was etched against the thin darkness of the room. Turning around, he called to his wife to get up, wake their son up and prepare some salted tea before it grew late.

His wife took the *kangri* out from under her *firan* and yawned. Opening the door, Hasandin took an armful of grass and climbed cautiously down the wooden step-ladder.

A small brook, a *nullah* flowed noiselessly down the middle of the lane. On one side stood wooden cabins raised on stilts for storing rice and on the other, two-storied shacks, angular and oddly shaped, their small compounds demarcated by picket fences. Hasandin dumped the hay in one corner of the compund. A large stone trough stood nearby, a permanent fixture which Hasandin had seen there ever since he was a toddler. People said it had taken his great grandfather two years to hew it out of a boulder and that he had used it to feed his horses. One could not find a bigger trough in the whole of Parezpur. But now Hasandin had three horses to look after—two of his own and one belonging to his brother. Since the trough was not big enough to feed three horses, the women of the house used it for thrashing paddy. And when they came into some extra money, they also ground salt and spices on its rough surface. In any case, the trough served as an identification mark for Hasandin's house and he was known in the village as Hasandin, of the big stone trough.

Resting one foot on the trough, Hasandin cast a fleeting glance at the narrow meandering lane and at the rickety houses silhouetted against the sky. He had heard at the Tangmarg pony-stand that the government proposed to demolish these shack-like affairs and have solid houses built in their stead—houses made of lime and bricks, with plastered walls and regular staircases. They would even be fitted with electricity. He doubted that such houses would ever come up in his own lifetime; the proposition seemed too good to be true. He had however heard that the people of Pehalgam were about to be served with a notice to vacate their village. The government would allot them some other suitable land two miles away free of cost, provide them with wood, and an advance of five hundred rupees each to construct new houses. The government wanted to utilize the vacated site for construction of small villas for tourists. The peasants were of course determined not to give up their ancestral houses. The scheme sounded fishy. The government alone, Hasandin thought, knew its mind or perhaps *rabbul-aalameen,* who belonged to all—the high and the low—and knew their minds. As for him, he was content with his existing house, old and rickety though it was. More than a proper house, he wanted work—work which brought him food.

He wished he could keep on standing by the brook, one foot resting on the trough, and beguile the time away conjuring up visions of the new house. But he was a matter-of-fact man, having neither the imagination nor the leisure to indulge in such fanciful thoughts. The only thing he knew was that he had to be on time at the pony-stand.

His wife came after him carrying a bundle of hay. 'Ya Allah!' Hasandin heaved a deep sigh and invoked that unseen power whom he made the repository of all his deeds and misdeeds, thus absolving himself of responsibility.

The horses started neighing at the smell of grass. '*Var, Var!*' Hasandin admonished them to have patience and climbed up the step-ladder again to fetch more grass.

His wife did not follow him. Instead, she proceeded to wake up Mamdoo who was sleeping in a corner of the stable. Mamdoo, a distant cousin, who had neither land nor a house of his own, looked after Hasandin's horses. In return, he was given food and shelter.

Hasandin's wife, still under thirty, had a fair complexion, sharp features, and a lovely name—Yasman. But her breasts sagged and hard work, perpetual hunger and a squalid life made her look older than her years. After she had taken out the horses with Mamdoo's help, she got down to cleaning the stable. In the meantime Hasandin had made three more trips with the grass.

The horses started munching. When his wife had gone upstairs, Hasandin came out and stood in the open gate. June was coming to a close and the nip in the air had lost its edge. As Hasandin looked at the rippling water, he thought of doing ablutions and saying his morning *namaz*. Strangely enough, though he had a blind faith in God, he was no stickler for *namaz* or for religious fasting. The daily grind hardly left him time to say the *namaz* five times a day as laid down by his religion. But the Lord of the Two Worlds knew and understood the plight of his followers. Didn't He know that poor Hasandin left the house at the break of dawn, harried himself all day taking the tourists around and returned home after nightfall, weary and worn out? He was convinced that his travails were known to the Almighty. That was the reason he contented himself by reciting the *kalma* and mumbling a hurried prayer before falling asleep every night.

The morning breeze was fresh and crisp, and the water of the brook inviting. Hasandin had a lot of time on hand. To what better use could he put it than by saying the morning *namaz* and earning merit?

Instructing Mamdoo to hurry up with his work, he proceeded towards the fields to answer the call of nature. Returning to the brook, he washed his hands and then scooping up water in his cupped hands, he sniffed at it three times. Three times he rinsed his mouth and then washed his face and fore-arms the same number of times. Then, cupping some water in his hands, he sprinkled it on the ground. With his wet palms he wiped his face, nose and forehead. Pushing back his hair, he put his fingers in his ears. Three times he washed first his right foot and then his left. After performing this ritual, he uncoiled the blanket from around his neck and spreading it on the ground, knelt down to say the morning *namaz*.

The darkness had become less opaque. A sombre sky peeped from behind the clouds. In the morning haze the wooden house of the shepherds of Parezpur looked melancholy. In deep winter, when the lower portions were hidden under snow, they did not look so seedy. But now the long wooden stilts on which these houses rested imparted a gloomier look. A couple of dogs, coming out of their resting places, roamed about like lost souls. Horses, let loose at night with their fore-legs tied together to graze in the fields, were now hopping back to the village. Parezpur was slowly coming to life. But Hasandin, oblivious of all this was lost in meditation. The *namaz* over, he spread out his hands invoking God's benediction: 'O Almighty! Listen to me, your humble creature. I am a sinner, but you are the forgiver; I am without work, but you can provide it. It's now many days that I have been denied a good customer, may my three horses be hired today. Please send me a good customer, one who will not only go upto Gulmarg, but upto Khilanmarg, and even beyond to Donala, so that I may recover my previous day's losses.'

TWO

God, it seemed, had heard Hasandin's prayer. When he reached the pony-stand at Tangmarg along with his son Idu and cousin Mamdoo, he saw to his great relief that Raina and Karim Khan were not there. Instead, Sardar Harnam Singh was strutting about, flourishing his baton—feeling quite important in his policeman's uniform. While absorbed in *namaz,* Hasandin might have momentarily forgotten his worry, but all the time he had been washing down the insipid *schyeru* with salted tea and while racing the horses towards Tangmarg, the worry, that Raina or Karim Khan might be on point-duty, had kept gnawing at his mind and he had silently prayed that Harnam Singh be on duty for the day.

'Salaam Huzoor!' he greeted Harnam Singh from a distance, gently bowing his head and baring his teeth in a smile.

'So you are up at the battle post, eh?' Harnam Singh said, brushing his bristly beard with his hand.

Harnam Singh was a Sikh, short-statured, lean and sinewy. He had neither the fair complexion that one often associated with Kashmiri Sikhs nor the shimmer of gold resembling the colour of unripe corncobs that one often observes in their hair. His face and hair were both jet-black like those of Punjabi Sikhs. He had not pressed his beard with a beard-band or twisted it round with a cord and it was as short as his stature. With his hollow cheeks and broad bony jaws, the untied and unfixed hair of his short beard gave his face a harsh expression. His staccato remark 'So you are up at the battle post, eh?' flung at Hasandin with a faint smile was meant to be a joke, but sounded more like a rebuke.

Hasandin smiled ingratiatingly and proceeded to tie up his horses at the pony-stand.

He was a poor peasant of Parezpur. A small plot of land, three horses and a ramshackle three-roomed house were all the property he owned in the world. He was no more than forty-five, but hard word and meagre food had already creased his face. Medium height, protruding jaws, sunken temples, yellow teeth, the upper lip shaved and only the tips of the moustache merging into the grey beard—he was always seen wearing a dirty Kashmiri *firan*. While tying the horses, he once again thanked God for having put Harnam Singh on duty, with whom he had a secret understanding. He might skimp the contractor's dues, but he dutifully paid Harnam Singh his fixed share. The constable often gave Hasandin a taste of his baton, but he also made it a point to assign him the most prosperous looking visitors.

After making obeisance to the policeman on duty, Hasandin went off to call on the owners of the two hotels and to have a word with the bearers, cooks and water carriers, who, Hasandin knew, had a big hand in tilting the wavering customer's decision in favour of one horse owner or the other. Having made the calls, he spread a blanket on the slope of the pony-stand and lay down in the sun.

He had hardly rested a few minutes, when he saw a bus coming in the distance. He sat up with a jerk and screwed up his eyes in a squint. It was a private bus. His companions scrambled to their feet and the coolies became alert. But Hasandin was not interested. Only the stingy type preferred to travel by private buses, so as to save some fare. They valued money more than comforts. The bulk of such visitors engaged coolies to carry their luggage and preferred to walk rather than ride. Hasandin always had his eyes on government buses.

The government bus also arrived soon after. There was a flurry of activity at the bus stand. The coolies stampeded to grab at the bed rolls, three coolies clinging to each bed roll. Anxious to establish their priorities, they thrust number-discs into the passenger's pockets, making it difficult for them to take down the luggage from the bus. When the luggage had been taken care of, the syces came forward. Some of the poor ones who did not own their horses but took them on contract mingled among the coolies.

Standing back from the crowd, Hasandin, with eagle eyes and knitted brows, tried to size up the passengers. Barefoot, wearing torn shirts or *firans,* dirt clinging to their bodies, the coolies swarmed around the bus and tore at one another like hungry dogs fighting for a piece of bone. Flourishing the baton over his head and mouthing choicest obscenities like a typical policeman, Harnam Singh rushed into the melee. He struck blindly at the coolies, as if they were not men but clods of earth.

The coolies scattered in a trice. Only those whom Harnam Singh wished to remain, or those who were resolute enough to defy the beating for the sake of a few *annas,* held their ground. Then Hasandin came forward with the other syces. His shrewd eye singled out a *seth*—a flabby young man of about thirty, fair with cheeks white as butter and wearing a silk shirt and corduroy pants. A woollen coat was resting on his arm. He was asking Harnam Singh the horse fare to Gulmarg and Khilanmarg. His wife and child stood a little away from him. Hasandin perked up his ears. He exchanged a meaningful glance with Harnam Singh on the sly.

'Sardarji, we want gentle horses,' Hasandin heard the *seth* saying. 'None of us is very good at riding.'

'Please go and have your tea,' Sardar Harnam Singh said, 'I'll have the horses sent over to you. If I have the time I'll bring them myself.'

The hotel guide was at hand. As the guide led the *seth* to the hotel, Hasandin winked at Harnam Singh and, with an imperceptible nod of the head, indicated that he would see Harnam Singh after fixing things with the *seth*. He then turned and followed the rich man at a respectable distance.

THREE

The hotel lawn commanded a good view of the Parezpur nullah against the backdrop of the mountains. The chairs and tables had been set up on the lawn, where the visitors could refresh themselves with tea and admire the scenic splendour of the mountains. The *seth*, his wife and child settled down at a table and ordered tea and toast.

Hasandin lingered on the verandah, keeping an eye on the prospective customers.

The *seth*'s wife said, 'Khanna Sahib, why not take a photograph while we are waiting for the tea?'

'Yes Papoji,' the boy cackled, distorting the word in his affection, 'Take two!' he got up from the chair and made a somersault on the lawn.

'An excellent idea!' Khanna Sahib (for that was the name of the *seth* in the silk shirt) got up from his chair.

Hasandin watched Khanna Sahib with interest as he took a small camera out of the leather bag hanging from his shoulder. He clicked a button and in the twinkling of an eye the small camera expanded into an oversized contraption. Next, he took a stand from his coat pocket and pulled out its three legs. Fitting the camera on the tripod, he threw a piece of black cloth over it.

Years ago, when the Britishers ruled Kashmir, Hasandin had seen a photographer at Gulmarg's Nido's Hotel taking the photograph of an English couple. Khanna Sahib must be a rich man. He hurried towards the pony shed where Sardar Harnam Singh was still strutting about dutifully waving his baton over the poor coolies.

Khanna Sahib took a couple of shots of the Parezpur nullah and then of the valley below. Meanwhile the tea came, and Khanna Sahib trained the camera on his wife and child as they proceeded to drink their tea. To give the photographs a realistic touch, he asked the child to hold a biscuit and the wife, a cup of tea. He was readjusting the cloth over the bellows of the camera when a bystander, who had come with Khanna Sahib on the same bus, asked him if he was a photographer.

'Oh no! I own a small cloth shop in Chandni Chowk, Delhi.' Khanna Sahib stopped tinkering with the camera and smiled.

'But your camera...'

'Oh, yes, it's an ordinary one. Brownie 620.'

'This black cloth....'

'You don't have to tell me,' Khanna Sahib cut in, 'It's quite old. In fact, a friend of mine bought it ages ago. Its bellows got spoiled for lack of use.'

'What's wrong with the bellows?'

'As you can see, it's riddled with tiny holes and light penetrates through them. I thought I would have it repaired at the Simla Studio in New Delhi. But I was so busy till the last minute that I clean forgot about it. In Srinagar I enquired at Mahatta's. They told me it would take a couple of days to repair it. As a make-shift arrangement they gave me this cloth. It works all right.'

Khanna Sahib smiled again and started puttering with the camera. After taking two snaps of his wife and child, he set the distance and aperture; then he went and sat down where his wife had been sitting and took a piece of toast in his hand while his wife went and clicked the shutter.

They had just finished with their tea when Hasandin arrived on the scene with Sardar Harnam Singh. The way he kept himself in the background, one would have got the impression that it was Harnam Singh who was responsible for bringing him there. Behind Hasandin came Idu and Mamdoo, holding the reins of the horses.

'Here they are!' Harnam Singh said effusively. 'Just the kind of horses you want. These men are quite reliable. When you left everything to me I had to be careful. I picked these three horses out of fifty odd horses here. The horses at the pony-stand are terrible—upto all sorts of tricks. But the ones I have selected are safe—even a child can ride them.'

Khanna Sahib thanked Harnam Singh and said that if all policemen discharged their duties as conscientiously as he, the tourists would be relieved of a good deal of worry.

'Look here, you!' Harnam Singh glared at Hasandin, 'Don't try to be clever with the gentleman. Take him to all the places he wants to visit.' Then he turned to Khanna Sahib and snapped out a smart 'Jai Hind', and departed.

Khanna Sahib wanted to have a look at the horses. 'No worry, Sa'b!' Hasandin said expansively. He had a horse brought forward for inspection. Holding the saddle, he helped Khanna Sahib mount the horse.

'It's a very gentle horse, Sa'b. If you let the rein loose, it will take you straight to Alpatthar.'

Khanna Sahib was satisfied and did not consider it necessary to inspect the other horses.

'And what about the luggage?' he asked, dismounting.

'The coolies will carry it, Sa'b. The rate is twelve *annas* per coolie. You can ask the policeman, Sa'b. It's the scheduled rate.'

Khanna Sahib's luggage consisted of two bed rolls, a suitcase and a canvas bag. He felt that one coolie could easily carry the entire load. When two coolies each took charge of a bed roll and a third one tied the suitcase and the canvas bag in a blanket, adjusted the load on his back and got ready to start, Khanna Sahib stopped the coolies and ran to Harnam Singh.

The policeman explained to him that it was a steep climb to Gulmarg. As it was, the bed rolls were quite heavy and the coolies would not be able to carry anything else. If the suitcase and the bag were not too big, the syces would agree to carry them for some extra money.

Acting on Harnam Singh's advice, Khanna Sahib dismissed the third coolie, asked Hasandin to carry the suitcase and told his son Idu to pick up the bag. He promised to pay them something extra for their labour.

Mamdoo had already gone ahead with Mrs Khanna. Idu was too young to carry loads. But Hasandin said with great bravado, 'Don't worry, Sa'b. I'll fix up everything.' He untied the blanket from around his neck and spreading it on the ground, wrapped the suitcase in it and put it on his shoulder.

'Here, pick up the bag,' he told his son.

Cutting across the bridle path, the two coolies had already taken the shorter route to Gulmarg. Khanna Sahib mounted his horse with Hasadin's help and they hurried after Mrs Khanna and their son.

They had gone only a short distance when Hasandin found Idu struggling with the bag. He took the bag from his son, tied it in the blanket along with the suitcase, and strapped it across his back the way Tibetan women carry their babies. When they resumed the journey, Hasandin's back was humped and he walked with a stoop.

As Hasandin plodded his way up the stiff, tortuous climb to Gulmarg, he again thanked Allah for having heard the prayers of an insignificant creature like himself; for having secured him a customer of his liking.

FOUR

'Var, Var!' Hasandin cautioned the horse not to break into a run. As he walked behind his horse carrying that heavy load, Hasandin made some quick calculations: if his customer made a round trip to Khilanmarg and paid him the scheduled rate, he would be richer by seventeen rupees. It could be even eighteen. Judging from his appearance, the *seth* looked quite affluent. He might shell out three or four rupees for the luggage. And if he could persuade the man to go upto Baba Rishi, he might rake in another seven or eight rupee. If after reaching Khilanmarg, the *seth* decided to see the frozen lake and visit Alpatthar, he could act as his guide and touch him for a small *bakshish*, not to mention the 'tea money'.

Mrs Khanna and the child had by now moved far ahead of Khanna Sahib. Striding forward Hasandin prodded the horse and it broke into a run. For some distance he kept pace with the horse and when it came abreast of the other horses, he slackened his pace and got lost in his thoughts.

Scenes of the past few years swiftly revolved before his mind. True, Hindustan had become independent and Pakistan had come into being, but the country's independence had given a setback to business in Kashmir. The land did not yield enough to feed the entire population. Even if the people managed somehow to make ends meet, they were not left with any money to invest in business and thus supplement their incomes. As always, tourism was the mainstay of the valley. Whatever their calling—whether fishermen or craftsmen, peasants or labourers, they depended on the tourist traffic for a living. And as it happened, tourism had become the first casualty of Independence. First came the *Pathan* hordes, who ransacked village after village, laying waste the country in their wild sweep, like a river in spate. When the tide swept back, Kashmir had become a vast morass in which the fish floundered about, trying to keep alive. Of course, there were a few puddles here and there, where the fish had the time of their life. The military units from India which were stationed in the cantonments brought some economic gain in their wake. But the military could not take the place of tourists. Hasandin's own village had to suffer a good deal. The other sources of income being totally closed to them, they had to fall back on the land. This helped them to have one or two daily meals, meagre though they were; but they got no yield from the land to sell in the market so as to fulfill their other equally important needs. It was, for instance the ardent desire of Hasandin's old mother that her grandson's and grand daughter's marriage be performed while she lived. She had invoked the blessings of Baba Pam Din, the great saint. But how could one think of marriage when he had not even sufficient food in the house?

Hasandin recalled a day, about eleven years ago, when they had gone with Idu to Bapam Rishi's tomb. The visit was a sequel to an earlier one. Although Hasandin had been married five years, he had not been blessed with a child. It was during that time that his mother took him to the tomb of Bapam Rishi. His wife had snipped a lock of her hair and tying it to the grill of the window, had taken a vow that if Bapam Rishi blessed her with a son she would dedicate him to the service of the saint. Next year Idu was born. Hasandin's mother wanted, in keeping with the vow, to offer the child to Baba Pam Din. But neither Hasandin nor his wife was keen to fall in with the old woman's wishes. It would give their hearts too great a wrench to part with such a pretty and healthy child. When the old woman warned them that the saint's wrath might befall them, they paid a hurried visit to the priest of the tomb. If the prophet Abraham could appease God by offering a lamb in lieu of his son, would not Baba Pam Din, they asked, accept a token offering in place of Idu? The priest told them that there was a way out in such cases. He advised them to leave one lock of hair on Idu's shorn head and not to touch it till Hasandin made good his vow. Hasandin left a lock of hair on the child's shorn head which was not to be cut off until Hasandin made good his vow. He was to sacrifice a sheep and distribute one hundred rupees in charity.

When Idu turned four, his grandmother again took him to Baba Rishi's tomb. The whole scene came back vividly to Hasandin's mind. Inside the mausoleum, the barber cut the lock from Idu's head and placed it at the foot of the tomb. Hasandin made an offering of one hundred rupees. Then they sacrificed a big fat lamb and put a large cauldron on the fire. Dancing round the cauldron in a circle, the women sang psalms in praise of the saint. They baked big flat *chapatis* and invited everyone to partake of the feast. The priest kept fifty rupees to himself and distributed the other fifty among the poor.

The ceremony cost Hasandin three hundred rupees. But living in those days was cheap. The British ruled over India and Gulmarg was their favourite hill resort—a paradise on earth. Every season

Hasandin managed to earn between four to five hundred rupees. After getting through the winter, which was the off season, he managed to save one hundred rupees, which he hid in the ground. At the end of three years, he was able to fulfil his vow at the tomb of Baba Rishi with great eclat. The same day Hasandin's mother tied a string round the window grill and vowed that if her elder son was blessed with a daughter she would have her married to Idu in the mausoleum of the saint. Hasandin's elder brother's wife gave birth to a daughter the following year. The old woman attributed the birth to the blessings of the saint. Idu was immediately betrothed to the new born girl. Despite all her wishes, the old woman did not live to see the blessed day of their marriage. Meanwhile India became free.

Hasandin's mother had darkly hinted that her daughter-in-law had sinned by not dedicating the first born to Baba Rishi. It was because of her reneging on her vow that she did not get another child, much less a son. She also attributed the calamity that had befallen Kashmir to this act of sinful omission.

Hasandin fell on evil days. He had to support a large family and, on top of that, he had to put up with his mother's taunts. He became querulous and flew off the handle at the slightest provocation. 'If Baba Rishi is angry why didn't he punish us that same year? Why after one year.' he shouted at his mother. 'Foolish woman! These things are beyond your understanding. You don't know a thing. If you hear our leader's speeches, you will know the real reason.'

Although he could not distinguish A from B, Hasandin had picked up a few ideas from the Englishmen whom he took around to Gulmarg, Khilanmarg, Alpatthar, Kantarnag and other places. He thought his mother stupid and superstitious and often chided her for it. All the same he had a sneaking fear that the saint was angry with him. His brother was blessed with four more sons, whereas his wife did not bear him a single child after Idu's birth.

'Ya Pir!' he suddenly moaned. 'Forgive me—a sinner.'

A riderless horse galloped past him.

'What's wrong with that horse?' Khanna Sahib asked, looking back from his saddle.

Before Hasandin could answer, a small boy ran past him in pursuit of the horse.

'It's that damn contractor's horse,' Hasandin said, 'It must have thrown off the rider.' He sidled upto Khanna Sahib and dropped his voice to a whisper. 'Sa'b, this contractor is a rascal, hand in glove with the officers. My horse, as you know, Sa'b, is my own. I don't allow servants to touch it, not even my son. I always keep a gentle horse.'

For a while he walked in silence. And then, as if talking to himself, he said, 'Sa'b, I did not have this horse in the beginning; I had another horse, but one day it threw off the rider and that was the end of it. I sold it the next day. A spirited horse won't do in these places. Mine is as docile as a lamb. If you let go its rein it will make a bee line to Alpatthar. I swear by Bapam Rishi, I never tell lies.'

'Are Bapam Rishi and Baba Rishi two different saints?'

'No, Sa'b, they are the names of the same saint. Some call him Bapam Rishi, others Baba Rishi. He is the patron saint of the Hindus and Muslims alike—the great Baba Pam Din.'

'You mean Payam-ud-din?'

'That's so, Sa'b.'

'I heard people mentioning his name in Srinagar. How far is his tomb from Gulmarg?'

'About seven miles going and coming. I can take you there today if you like.'

Khanna Sahib dropped the topic, but Hasandin again picked up the thread after a while.

'He is a great saint—Baba Pam Din,' Hasandin said, catching up with the horse and walking swiftly, although bent double under the load. 'He held a high post in the times of the Mughals. He was held in high esteem at the Royal court and the Mughal Emperor gave him one thousand gold mohurs. It was his habit to go out for a ride every day. One day, as the story goes, he felt like walking and got down from his horse. As he was walking, he saw a long line of ants busy laying in stock for the winter. It suddenly occurred to him that even such petty creatures as ants thought of the future, whereas man—the highest creation of God—was quite oblivious of it. He did nothing to earn merit for the next world. Baba Pam Din cursed himself for his worthless life. He immediately retraced his steps, gave up his title at the court, bade farewell to the family, and, going to Aish Mukam, fell at the feet of Zain Baba. He spent long years in meditation and learnt the ways of God. One day Zain Baba said to him, "Son! There's nothing more I can teach you. You had better go elsewhere." Baba Sahib then left Aish Mukam, became a recluse, and lived in a jungle where he meditated on God. In a short time his fame spread all over Kashmir, and people came from distant places to sit at his feet. As it happened, at the time he left the court, his wife was expecting and a son was born to her. When the son grew up, he went in search of his father and happened to pass through the jungle. The Baba was pleased to meet his son and instructed him to retire to a lonely spot and spend his life in meditation of the Supreme. Well, as you know, the son was a young man given to the luxuries of the city. To expect him to live as a hermit was asking too much. He fell in with evil company. When the reports of his misdeeds reached his father, the man was beside himself with indignation. He prayed to God to put an end to his son's wicked existence. The Baba was a great fakir, dear to Him. How could god ignore his prayer? He called away his son unto Himself.'

Hasandin walked some distance in silence and then said, 'Sa'b, I have never heard of Baba Rishi refusing a prayer. People come from distant places to visit his tomb.'

'I have heard that the chief minister visits his tomb.'

'You are right, Sa'b. And he has ordered that electricity be installed in the tomb.'

They had reached the spot where the horse had thrown off the rider, and saw two men walking along supporting a young, rather fat girl between them, their horses following.

'Did she fall from the horse?' Khanna Sahib asked, coming abreast of the party.

'Yes,' the middle aged man accompanying the girl replied. 'The government should take such horses off the route.'

And Khanna Sahib turned towards Hasandin and said, 'We'll go to see all the places only on your horse.'

'Don't worry, Sa'b, I'll take you wherever you want to go. I'll show you the whole of Gulmarg and if Sa'b wants to do Khilanmarg, I'll also take you there. Afrabat, Alpatthar and even the frozen lake. Wherever Sa'b wishes to go, Hasandin will go with you.'

'Do they sacrifice goats at the tomb of Baba Rishi?' Khanna Sahib's mind was still not free of the saint.

'Yes, *sarkar*! You see this little boy Idu, my son. He was born because of Baba Rishi's blessings. I sacrificed a sheep and distributed one hundred rupees in charity.'

Khanna Sahib, a bania by caste, did not like the sacrifice part. 'Is it necessary to slaughter a goat?' he asked.

'No, Sa'b. Only the Muslims sacrifice animals. The Hindus

offer fruits and sweets and give money in charity. Whatever the offering, half of it goes to the tomb, and the other half is distributed among the poor.'

Khanna Sahib's mind was made up. 'All right, Hasandin,' he said with an air of finality, 'We'll visit Baba Rishi's tomb.'

FIVE

The last lap of the ascent to Gulmarg had started.

The horses slowed down and those who trudged behind them laboriously worked their way up.

Unable to keep pace with the horse, Hasandin again fell behind. When the horse stopped to champ at the grass growing in the crevices, Hasandin would emerge from the inner world of his dreams, urge the horse on and again lapse into thought.

He was pleased at having been able to prevail upon Khanna Sahib to visit Baba Rishi's tomb. Hasandin made some quick calculations again—from Tangmarg to Gulmarg and then on to Baba Rishi and back—the trip would fetch him at least thirty rupees. And if he could manage to take Khanna Sahib upto Alpatthar and the frozen lake it would mean another five rupees. He almost choked with joy. Suddenly it occurred to him that if Khanna Sahib decided to prolong the stay at Gulmarg, he was likely to engage some other horses for the return trip. But how could that be? He quickly dismissed the thought. I'll serve him so well that he won't think of engaging other horses.

But despite his self assurance he took a few brisk strides and, panting between breaths, asked, '*Seth*! How many days do you intend staying in Gulmarg?'

In bygone days, he would have asked in terms of weeks and months, but now Gulmarg lay almost desolate. If the place was still a big draw, it was because of its past glory. Now visitors came just to have a look at the place, stayed for a day or two, at the most a week and then departed.

'I'll go back tomorrow,' Khanna Sahib said. 'I'm in a hurry. From Gulmarg I'll go to Pehalgam and then make the pilgrimage to Amarnath.'

Hasandin fell back again. He was happy that the *seth* would spend only one day at Gulmarg, and thanked God from the bottom of his heart for having heard his prayer. The morning prayer, he knew, had great significance. God responded to it more than any other prayer. He had also heard old men saying that a curse or a prayer uttered at a fateful moment came true word for word. That was why one was cautioned to carefully weigh his words before uttering them. Accordingly, if he had asked for something more substantial this morning, say a lakh of rupees, his wish would have been granted.

Hasandin was carried away by his imagination. He imagined that he is saying his morning *namaz* and has asked God for a lakh of rupees. Then the scene shifts to his stable, where he is digging a corner to set up a pole for the door. As he digs the earth, his spade strikes against something brittle. He digs on feverishly and discovers that it is a bronze jar. He hastily covers up the hole, fearing that Mamdoo or a neighbour might get scent of his precious find. As the day advances he asks his wife to help him put up a curtain across the stable. On some pretext he sends Mamdoo upstairs to sleep.

At midnight, when the village is asleep, he comes downstairs with his wife, who carries a hurricane lantern. This time they do not dig near the door as it is close to the lane, but inside at the other end of the stable. The subconscious mind obligingly plays tricks to suit the convenience of the daydreamer; in this respect, dreams of the night or the day are similar in their working. After digging patiently, taking care that the sound did not carry outside, both of them lift the jar out of the hole. The lid is sealed with shellac. They remove the lid. Their eyes widen in astonishment—the jar is full of gold *mohurs*, which dazzle the eyes even in the dim light of the hurricane lantern. Hasandin picks up a handful of coins and, holding out his hand slowly, opens it in front of his wife who, in her excitement to have a closer look at the coins, raises the lantern. As they stand looking at the coins delirious with joy and apprehension at such an unbelievable find, they hear a soft noise. They look around, startled. They find Mamdoo standing at the door. As their eyes meet, he bares his teeth in a smile. In his trepidation, Hasandin lets Mamdoo in on the secret and tells him that he would share the precious find equally with all the members of the family. Now that God had been kind to them, it is incumbent upon them not to forget the horses that have stood by them in their hours of joys and sorrows. Keeping their past services in mind, the horses would not be put to work any more and a servant would be engaged to look after them. Hasandin then tells them that he would like to set apart an equal share for each horse. As he speaks, Hasandin's face shines with a divine glow.

It is here that Mamdoo's cussedness comes to the surface. He refuses to share the *mohurs* with the horses, whereas Hasandin insists upon dividing the coins equally among the members of the family and the horses, giving one share to Mamdoo. But Mamdoo is adamant. He wants a fourth of the whole lot. At last Hasandin tries to compromise by giving him one horse and its share of coins in addition. But the very Mamdoo who did not dare bat an eye at his uncle, now kicks up a row and abuses him roundly. Meanwhile someone has reported the matter to the police, who crashes down upon them like an avalanche. Not only do they carry away the jar, but they arrest the family into the bargain....

....Hasandin was breathing heavily. Beads of sweat had broken out on his forehead. The horse had stopped near a precipice and was merrily devouring the wayside shrubs. Khanna Sahib, afraid of falling, was pulling wildly at the reins. Breaking a thin branch from a tree, Hasandin ran forward, brandishing it in the air and mouthing profanities. But before he could whip the horse, it had resumed its journey.

Hasandin adjusted the load on his back and followed the horse. His mind was at work spinning out another yarn....

....This time Mamdoo and Idu are away in Kantarnag with the horses. Being unwell, he has stayed back, and his elder brother has gone out in his place. To while away the time, he has just started working in the stable when his spade strikes against the jar. In the dead of night he and his wife remove the coins from the jar and hide them in two and threes in different places under the thatched roof. Hasandin, whose illness has vanished at the sight of the coins, goes to Tangmarg the next day and brings back bottles of wine and heaps of delicacies. He invites his old mother, his brother and his family, and a few neighbours to his house. While the men enjoy the wine, the women drink coffee in place of salted tea and eat fine *scheyrus* and bread cooked in milk. All have the time of their lives, feasting late into the night. Suddenly two cats start fighting and jumping on the roof, raising a hell of a noise. The gold coins are dislodged and come tumbling down on the floor. Word goes round that Hasandin's roof is raining gold. And then, like destiny, the police appear on the scene. They pull apart every straw of the roof, take possession of the coins, and arrest all the members of the family. In the end, Hasandin has to sell off all the walnut-crammed boxes in order to bribe the police and stop the law from taking its course....

....Hasandin jerked his head. But the subconscious mind had not finished its reverie. This time it came out with a slightly different version: there is not one but two jars. He hides one in a safe place. Covering the hole with earth, he spreads hay over it and ties a horse near it. He then goes to the revenue officer of Tangmarg and reports finding a treasure. The officer comes to his house and recovers the jar containing the coins. Not satisfied, the officer orders the constables to dig up the whole floor and make a thorough search. The earth where Hasandin had dug up the second jar is still loose. The rest is clear enough—Hasandin is beaten black and blue and his wife, fearing that her husband might die, tells the police everything about the second jar. The police haul him up for theft....

....Hasandin shook his head violently. He lost his treasure every time. He tried to hold fast to his booty like a kitten trying to catch a big chameleon, but it always slipped through his fingers. Leave alone one lakh, he had never seen even a thousand rupees. As for gold *mohurs*, his forefathers might have seen them, but he had just heard about them. Even in his dreams he was not able to hold on to them.

With a jerk of the head, he accelerated his pace. The climb was over. Their way now lay through a patch of green with a couple of *deodars* growing on its fringes. The horses ahead of Khanna Sahib had stopped in the grove for a breather.

'Why have we stopped here?' Khanna Sahib turned and asked Hasandin.

'The horses pause here awhile to regain their breath,' Hasandin said putting down his load. 'Just touch the horse. It's drenched with sweat.'

SIX

Khanna Sahib inadvertently patted the side of the horse. His hand became wet with perspiration.

'Hasandin, help me dismount,' he said wiping his hand against his corduroy pants.

'No need to get down, Sa'b. We'll start in a few minutes.'

But Khanna Sahib insisted upon getting down.

Hasandin gave him his shoulder; Khanna Sahib got down and walked over to his wife and son.

'Well, Shakun! You're not tired I hope?' he said to his wife and then, without waiting for an answer, turned to his son. 'And you, Kukku?' putting his hands under the child's arms he bounced him affectionately a few times and then kissed him.

'Not a bit, Papoji.' The child started frisking about like a colt.

Khanna Sahib liked this form of address. The word 'papoji' had more affection in it than 'papaji' or a mere 'papa'.

'Watch out child! Don't go behind the horse. It may kick you.' Hasandin ran forward and caught the child by the arm. Releasing himself, the child scampered off in the other direction.

Hasandin stood looking at the child, fascinated. Idu, his own son, was just this boy's age, may be a year or two older. But he was not born under a lucky star. From his very childhood he had to earn his keep. If conditions remained peaceful, he thought, he would perform Idu's marriage and have his children properly educated. He suddenly remembered the English visitors who had come there last year. When they addressed their parents as 'mummy' and 'daddy' or 'mama' and 'papa,' he hardly took notice of this. But now hundreds of nondescript Indians, many of them petty shopkeepers, visited Kashmir. They were contemptuously dubbed as *'Dal-i-visitor'* by the Kashmiris, for they ate nothing but rice and *dal*, never hired a horse, and trudged their way through Kashmir on foot, enjoying its heavenly beauty almost gratis. And yet their children addressed them as 'mummy'or 'daddy,' 'mama' or 'papa.' So, it had occurred to him, why shouldn't Idu address him as 'daddy' instead of 'abba.' Last year he told the boy to do so in the presence of Yasman, his wife.

Both Idu and Yasman had looked at him blankly, not comprehending what he meant. When Yasman realized his meaning, she guffawed loudly. 'Tomorrow you'll ask me to smear my face with powder and rouge,' she'd said, 'and go about half dressed like those city witches.'… And Idu had never called him 'daddy'.

Hasandin smiled to himself, but then his face suddenly became grave as he looked at Khanna Sahib's son frisking about. Some day, when Idu's sons went to school, they would learn to address their father as 'daddy'. He had himself wasted his life working like a beast of burden, but Idu's sons would have the good fortune of leading a decent life.

Then he realized that, instead of building castles in the air, he should come to grip with the realities of the moment. He must find out from the visitors if any of them were bound for Alpatthar or the frozen lake. It was his experience that one tourist often took his cue from another.

But none of the tourists, whose horses were now resting in the grove, had Alpatthar or the frozen lake on his itinerary. One of them was a trader, come to explore the possibilities of business at Gulmarg. Two were government employees. There were only two vacationers, but they intended to stay at Gulmarg for a week and then push on to Khilanmarg. Hasandin ferreted out this information from their syces.

Hasandin turned back. He was about to ask Khanna Sahib to mount his horse when he saw the tour party whose girl had fallen from the horse, coming up the slope. The girl was evidently riding another horse and was now ahead of the others. The middle-aged man in a suit rode the other horse. The youth, on foot, made up the rear.

'I hope she wasn't hurt,' Khanna Sahib said.

'Oh, no. She had a narrow escape,' the man in the suit replied. The girl blushed.

'How many days will you stay at Gulmarg?'

'Say, about four or five days.'

'We'll go back tomorrow.' Khanna Sahib said, 'I can't take more than a month off from my shop. But in a month, one can't do justice to even a corner of Kashmir.'

Khanna Sahib proceeded towards his horse. He was about to put his foot in the stirrup when he suddenly stopped. 'In which hotel will you be staying, Mr . . . ?' He stopped abruptly and looked at the elderly gentleman.

'Well, you can call me Uppal—Ved Vyas Uppal! We've not made up our minds. We'll decide when we get there. There's the

Gulmarg Hotel—and the Khalsa Hotel. I'm told they also rent out rooms in the bazaar.'

'I've decided to stay at the Khalsa Hotel.' With Hasandin's help Khanna Sahib heaved himself up into the saddle. Mr Uppal's party moved on soon after. The young man, as before, brought up the rear. Hasandin had been listening intently to their talk. After walking some distance, he caught up with the young man. 'Sa'b, are you coming from Delhi?'

'Yes, but I don't live there.'

'Where do you live? Bombay? Or is it Calcutta?'

'No, I have come from Africa.'

'Africa! Is Africa a part of America?'

'Africa lies between India and America—the Negro land.'

Hasandin cast a quick glance at the young man and then said hesitantly, 'But you look very much like an Indian.'

'Yes, of course I am an Indian. My grandfather migrated to Africa and settled there. We run our own business. I've come to see India.'

'What places have you visited in Kashmir?'

'We've just come here. In Srinagar, I saw the Dal and the Nagina lakes, the Shalimar and Nishat Gardens. We stop at Gulmarg for three days and then we'll be off to Pehalgam.'

Here was the opening that Hasandin had been waiting for. 'Gulmarg, as you know, Sa'b, is the best place in Kashmir—a paradise on earth. The frontier tribesmen plundered the whole place and carried away everything with them. But they couldn't carry away its beauty. Not even bandits can do that. Afrabat, Alpatthar, the frozen lake—Sa'b, people come from far off places to visit them. Only two days ago, four foreigners came here. They have now gone to Kantarnag and Tos-e-Maidan. Sa'b, now that you have come as far as Gulmarg, you must also visit the shrine of Baba Rishi, Parezpur Nullah, Khilanmarg, Afrabat, Alpatthar and the frozen lake. My Sa'b will move down tomorrow. I'll be free to take you around anywhere you like. My horse, Sa'b, is the last word in docility.'

'Is your Sa'b going to Alpatthar and the frozen lake?'

'I'm not sure, Sa'b. He said he would like to visit Baba Rishi. He may even go upto Khilanmarg. He may also visit other places if he can get the right company.'

'We are thinking of going to Khilanmarg tomorrow.'

'Sa'b, if you want to go to Afrabat and the frozen lake you must set out early in the morning so as to reach the top by noon. Oh, what a magnificent view the hill commands. You'll be thrilled to the core. *Sarkar*, if my Sa'b decides to go up I'll take you upto the frozen lake. I also act as a guide.'

Hasandin was trying to settle this business with his prospective customer when a boy came galloping up on a horse and dismounted before them.

'I refuse to ride your horse,' the young man said, brushing aside the boy.

'It's not the same horse Sa'b,' the boy said. 'It's very gentle. The other I left behind at the pony-stand.'

'No, I'd rather walk. Now that I have walked this far, I can just as well walk the rest of the distance.'

'Sa'b, you still have a long way to go. You've no idea of the distance, Sa'b. I'll be ruined. The contractor will deduct my wages. I am a poor boy.'

The boy fell at the young man's feet. The horse stood still, not even attempting to nibble at the shrubs. The young man glanced first at the boy cringing at his feet and then at the horse. Both looked so wretched that he caught hold of the rein without a word and mounted the horse. The horse which had looked so decrepit that it hardly seemed capable of taking a step suddenly broke into a run.

'Var, Var!' The boy scampered after the horse, warning it to slow down. But by now it had joined the other horses.

Hasandin again adjusted the load on his back and resumed his journey.

Whoever comes to Gulmarg invariably visits Pehalgam, Hasandin said to himself. If he stays at Gulmarg for two days, he'll stay at Pehalgam for two months. The syces and peasants of Pehalgam have a nice time of it. The real visitors of Gulmarg, who made the place what it is, are gone across the seven seas. Now only Indians frequent the place. And what Indians! They catch a chill even in the bracing climate of Gulmarg and the dread of pneumonia constantly stalks them.

But why blame them? Hasandin argued with himself. What charm does Gulmarg have for visitors? Not a single good shop, no hotel worth the name, no doctors, no hospital. Of course, there was the Nido's Hotel. But not everyone could afford to live in such a posh hotel. And as for Pehalgam—well, it had no peer among hill stations. It was the nodal point from which roads took off to all directions—to Chandanvari, Sheshnag, and Amarnath. This was also the starting point for Adu, Lidderwat. Kolohai Glacier, Tuliyan and the numerous other lakes. The bank of the Liddar—what a magnificent spot! The visitors pitched their tents and had a glorious time. If Gulmarg was the Englishman's paradise, Pehalgam was the Indian's heaven.

The year peace returned to Kashmir, tourist traffic picked up and three thousand pilgrims made the trip to holy Amarnath. Hasandin had been sure that the number would swell to five thousand next year. He thought of shifting his venue to Pehalgam. He could thereby earn a lot more during the season and then return home to spend the winter in comfort. At the start of the next season, he revealed his plan to his mother. She strongly disapproved of it.

'Son,' she said, 'when the fish spawn, God provides them with food in the same pond. If all the horsemen should take it into their hands to shift to Pehalgam, they would compete among themselves and all would starve. If Pehalgam lies on the route to Amarnath, Gulmarg has its Baba Rishi. Baba Rishi is as big a draw as Amarnath.'

Hasandin was impressed. He stayed where he was and his mother's words came true. The season improved and Bakshi Sahib had had two government shops opened here. But it wasn't just this. He had his own fields to look after. Trees of walnut, apricot and peaches. It was not for the women to pick the fruit and sell them in the market. While it was true that his brother chipped in, yet it was not one man's job.... Suddenly scenes of the past few years revolved before his mind, when due to the attacks of the frontier tribesmen, the number of visitors had dwindled to a trickle. The family was reduced to such dire straits that it had to subsist on the walnuts, peaches and apricots that grew in Hasandin's small plot of land. One could survive without new clothes, but the belly had to be filled.

But now imports of rice, wheat and other grains from India had started again and the trees were laden with fruit in luxurious abundance. Last year Hasandin had sold twenty-five rupees worth of walnuts, and this year he hoped to sell fifty. His boxes lay filled to the brim with walnuts. Besides, he could earn another twenty five rupees from the sale of other fruit. If he could earn about three hundred rupees during the season, he would set apart one hundred for the winter and spend the rest on Idu's marriage.

Suddenly he heard his name being shouted. It was Khanna Sahib. The horse had stopped and was now busy munching at the wayside bushes while Khanna Sahib tugged wildly at the reins. One could hear his frightened voice. 'Hasandin. Has-s-an-din!'

'Don't get scared, Sa'b. You won't fall. Just throw your weight backward!' Hasandin shouted from a distance.

'What do you mean? Throw your weight backward?' Khanna Sahib shouted back angrily. 'Why don't you walk by my side? Can't you see how far the others have gone? What kind of horse is this? It keeps stopping all the time.

'Sa'b, believe me, it's a very gentle horse.' Hasandin said in a conciliatory tone. 'But an animal is an animal. It can't resist the sight of grass. Spur it and it will start galloping.'

Hasandin swished the birch in the air. Khanna Sahib dug his heels into the horse's sides. The horse leaped forward. Khanna Sahib pulled hard at the rein.

'Var, Var!' Hasandin cried.

The horse slowed down. Khanna Sahib had started panting with the mild exertion. 'See how far those people have gone,' he said between his breaths. 'But this horse of yours won't budge an inch without you.'

'Don't be frightened, Sa'b. I'm with you now. We're on the last lap of the climb and we'll soon reach Gulmarg. Except for this heavy load, I'd have led the horse myself.' And edging forward, Hasandin caught hold of the rein.

SEVEN

When they reached the top, Khanna Sahib asked Hasandin to stop for a while at the circular road which girdled the place like a levee surrounding a deep lake. Right in front of him stretched the paddy-green valley of Gulmarg—a broad sloping sweep of grass creating the illusion of a vast green saucer. The yellow building at the base of the saucer, and the long row of frail wooden shops, smug in their sameness, which stretched in a row to the right, made the saucer look even bigger.

'Where's the Khalsa Hotel?'

Hasandin pointed towards a seedy looking yellow building which looked like a stale left-over in the vast saucer. Khanna Sahib's inquisitive gaze roved over the scene and then came to rest nearby on a squat, barrack-like building, enclosed by a small garden. A shallow brook, its bed flat as a sheet, ran along the edge of the garden. A sign-board obligingly announced—Gulmarg Hotel.

'Sa'b, it's just the place for you,' Hasandin said following Khanna Sahib's gaze. 'The cook is from Delhi. It offers better food than the Khalsa Hotel.'

'I'll stay at the Khalsa Hotel,' Khanna Sahib said sharply. But his wife and child were already at the gate, and the coolies, resting their loads against the neck-high compound wall were smoking *biris*. Some other visitors had gone in and were being shown the rooms.

'Let's go,' Khanna Sahib said. They proceeded towards the Gulmarg Hotel.

'It's a beautiful place,' Mrs Khanna said as her husband and Hasandin approached the gate.

'Beautiful no doubt, but probably equally expensive,' her husband snapped. 'We ought to find out the charges at the other hotel.'

'But Sa'b, you are staying here only for a day.' Hasandin ventured to add.

'I don't care if it's for a day or an hour.' Khanna Sahib said testily. 'I don't mind spending a thousand rupees at one shot, but I must know what I'm getting in return. Of course, these subtleties won't penetrate your thick skull.'

And indeed, Khanna Sahib's quirk of thought had left Hasandin wondering!

Before Khanna Sahib could descend the path to the Khalsa Hotel, he ran into Uppal Sahib, who had engaged a room and had come to have his luggage taken in.

'Well, have you decided upon this hotel?' Khanna Sahib asked.

'Yes, Usha would like to visit Baba Rishi, and we must get some food ready to take with us. There are only two hotels, each as good or as bad as the other.'

Khanna Sahib stood gazing at the brook, its bed rippling like a sheet of white cloth under the transparent water. The view pleased him, but he was still undecided. 'I've heard they let out rooms in the bazaar,' he said.

'Yes, there are one or two Sikh *dhabas* in the bazaar,' Uppal Sahib said. 'They let out rooms upstairs. But they are awful—like the dingy rooms of the *dhabas* at Batot, always filled with smoke. Even in the Rest House at Batot I had to put up in a tent. And a terrible time we had of it. I couldn't sleep the whole night. Well, Usha wants to go to Baba Rishi. If we spend any more time looking for rooms we'll have no time left to make the trip. And he walked off behind the coolies.

Khanna Sahib could not make up his mind. 'I also want to visit Baba Rishi,' he said turning to Hasandin. 'But I must see the other hotel first.'

'Sa'b, have a look at this place also,' Hasandin suggested. 'I assure you it's no way more expensive than the other hotel. If you don't like it here we shall go to the Khalsa Hotel.'

Hasandin was getting worried. Great God! If Khanna Sahib spent the whole time checking on hotel rooms, he might not even go to Donala, what to say of Alpatthar!

And he silently mumbled a prayer.

Khanna Sahib liked Hasandin's suggestion. Telling his wife and the child to remain in their saddles, he dismounted from his horse with the help of Hasandin's shoulder and proceeded towards the hotel. Untying the knot of the blanket, Hasandin deposited the suitcase and the canvas bag on the compound wall, threw the blanket around his neck, and hastened after Khanna Sahib. Walking through the small garden, and of course, not forgetting to take a quick look at the silver bed of the shallow brook as he crossed the wooden bridge, Khanna Sahib climbed the steps of the verandah. Hasandin went in and came hurrying back with the bearer.

Across the verandah, overlooking the brook, Rooms 3 and 4 were lying vacant. Khanna Sahib decided to inspect Room 3 first. It was of modest proportions, with an attached bathroom and its wooden floor covered with a grimy cotton carpet. A charpoy lay by the fireplace and another stood against the wall. The room also boasted of a small side table and a rickety armchair. The bathroom, perhaps because it was devoid of all modern fixtures, looked more spacious than the room.

Room 4 could hold only one charpoy and its bathroom was also smaller. The rent? Four rupees a day for Room 3, and rupees three for Room 4.

Khanna Sahib felt reassured. His friends at Srinagar had told him that rents at the Khalsa Hotel ranged between three and four rupees a day. It was against his code of business, however, not to haggle over a deal. He offered two rupees for Room 3 and one rupee for Room 4.

Casting a scornful glance at Khanna Sahib, the bearer walked away quietly.

'What kind of a customer is this?' Hasandin thought for a flash. Then he consoled himself with the thought that, though the days of British rule were over and the country had become independent, her people had not sloughed off their age old mentality. It had become second nature even with the most affluent visitor to drive a hard bargain. Hasandin's experience of the past three years had made him wiser. Glossing over Khanna Sahib's niggardly propensities, he told him that even if he roamed all over for hours, he wouldn't be able to get a cheaper room. Of course, he could secure some make-shift accommodation at one of the Sikh *dhabas*, but his wife and child wouldn't feel comfortable there. For one thing, there being no privy, they would have to go out in the freezing cold to answer the call of nature. 'Anyway, I'll sound out the bearer again in case he's willing to reduce the rent.'

The bearer's contemptuous look had galled Khanna Sahib, making him feel small before his syce. He jumped at Hasandin's proposal. Ultimately, Hasandin prevailed upon the bearer to reduce the rent by one rupee.

'Which room would you like to occupy, Sa'b?' Hasandin asked triumphantly.

'Room 4.'

Hasandin gasped in surprise. 'But there's only one cot in Room 4,' he said. 'What about your wife and the child? They'll be uncomfortable!'

Khanna Sahib had pulled up a chair by the edge of the brook and was now comfortably ensconced in it. He caught the note of surprise in Hasandin's voice. 'Never mind the cot!' he said with forced good humour. 'We can manage with it. We regard a visit to the hills as nothing more than a long picnic. It will be fun sleeping on the floor.'

'But it's very cold over here, Sa'b. The child may catch a chill.'

Just then the bearer appeared. To counteract the sneer that still lingered on the bearer's face, Khanna Sahib waved his hand in the air with casual indifference. 'Well, then take any room,' he said. 'Take Room 3. It makes no difference to me either way. Go and fetch Mrs Khanna and the child. I'll be here.'

'I've engaged Room number 3,' he shouted from where he sat as Mrs Khanna sailed in, coolie with the luggage in tow. He yawned.

Mrs Khanna swept into the room like a queen making a state entry into her royal domain. She puttered about as the coolies struggled with the luggage and then proceeded to unfasten the bed rolls.

Mrs Khanna went out into the verandah and asked her husband, 'What's the rent for this room?'

'Three rupees.'

'Couldn't we have a cheaper one?'

'We could take Room number 4 for two rupees. But it can't hold two cots. One of us would have to sleep on the floor.'

'Well, so what? What's the fun in coming to the hills if one can't sleep on the floor?'

'The place is very cold and we have to think of the child. We mustn't take any risk.' He looked sharply around to make sure that Hasandin was out of hearing. He was hanging around in the distance, waiting for the opportunity to broach the subject of going to Baba Rishi.

Mrs Khanna went back to the room. Khanna Sahib paid off the coolies and settled down to regale himself with the sight of the silver-bedded brook. The child came and sat down by his side.

'Papoji, won't you take our pictures?' he said snuggling closer.

'Yes, of course,' Khanna Sahib said expansively. 'Wait till your mummy comes.'

The child got up and went over to Uppal Sahib, who was standing on the verandah outside his room. He caught hold of his hand and brought him over to his father.

'Hello, won't you sit down?' Khanna Sahib said pushing a chair towards Mr Uppal.

In the course of the conversation Khanna Sahib pieced together information about Mr Uppal. He was teaching in a college at Delhi. The woman accompanying him was his niece. (Khanna Sahib had thought her a second wife, whom, Prof Uppal had probably married

late in life, for the woman looked about thirty.) She had recently
done her B.A. As she had been keeping poor health, Prof Uppal had
brought her with him to Kashmir for a change of climate.

'And the young man—is he related to you?'

'Oh, no.' Prof Uppal said. 'He's a nice young man that we met
in Srinagar. We rented a houseboat together. We were coming to
Gulmarg, so he said he would also join us.' Prof Uppal paused and
then asked Khanna Sahib if he intended to visit Baba Rishi.

'Yes, I've a good mind to,' Khanna Sahib said.

'I was wondering what to do about food. Will you take something
with you or buy it there? I hear there's a beautiful spring near the
shrine. Nice spot for a picnic. We may as well take a *durrie* with
us.'

Khanna Sahib nodded in approval.

'Then I'll have some sandwiches made. And you...?'

'Oh, don't worry about us. We had a heavy breakfast at
Tangmarg, and besides, we have some *parathas* with us.'

Prof Uppal left. Khanna Sahib shifted in the chair and turned
his back on him.

'I have no desire for these wretched sandwiches,' Khanna Sahib
said as if speaking to himself. 'They taste like paper. Who would care
to eat sandwiches when he can have delicious *parathas* dripping
with pure *ghee*?' And he chuckled to himself.

Hasandin had seen Englishmen eating egg or cheese sandwiches
on picnics. He had himself had the opportunity to taste them and
found them delicious—far tastier than the rice or maize *chapatis* and
schyeroos which he generally ate. But seeing Khanna Sahib laugh, he
also laughed good humouredly, as if corroborating Khanna Sahib's
statement. Then he went away to tell Idu and Mamdoo that Khanna
Sahib would soon be ready to start for Baba Rishi.

EIGHT

They were about to leave when Professor Uppal reminded Usha to take a *durrie* with her.

'Sa'b, you'll also do well to take a *durrie* with you,' Hasandin said to Khanna Sahib.

'Why? For what?'

'Just to sit on—for Me'm Sa'b and the child to rest on.'

'Don't we have grass there?'

'The place is very green, but…'

'Then we can do without a *durrie*. In fact, I don't believe in these flummeries. At home sleep on mattresses, but when the time comes don't hesitate to sleep on the bare ground—that's what I teach my son.'

Prof Uppal and his party had already preceded Khanna Sahib's. After seeing his wife and the child into the saddle, he heaved himself up on the horse with Hasandin's help.

Cutting across the maidan, they made a detour of the bazaar and took the upper road. Hasandin showed him the remnants of some tumble-down shops which the frontier tribesmen had looted and

then set on fire. The snowfall during the past three years had done
the rest; the ruins were now level with the ground.

'Didn't it snow here before?'

'It did, Sa'b. It snowed heavily. But the snow was cleared up from
the rooftops every year. When Gulmarg was ransacked and the
fighting broke out, the place was abandoned. The visitors stopped
coming here and the shops tumbled down.'

Hasandin remembered those harrowing days when a detachment
of tribesmen cut itself off from the main horde marching from
Baramula to Srinagar and took the road to Gulmarg. They had taken
complete possession of both the places and ultimately departed
with five hundred truckloads of booty.

At the end of the deserted bazaar a narrow path dipped towards
Baba Rishi. Khanna Sahib instructed Hasandin to hold the rein
and lead the horse. He shouted similar instructions to Idu and
Mamdoo.

'Don't worry, Sa'b. When the horse goes down the slope, you
lean backward.' As an extra measure of precaution, Hasandin sidled
up and took hold of the rein.

Suddenly Khanna Sahib struck an odd note by broaching
the topic of the sandwiches again. 'Do you know what we take
on picnics in Delhi?' Khanna Sahib paused long enough to give
Hasandin a fair chance to make a guess. Hasandin made no answer.
He cast a quick glance at Khanna Sahib, and continued to walk
along holding the horse's rein.

'Not these limp sandwiches and wretched jams, that's for
sure.' Khanna Sahib said exultantly. 'Oh no. We take *parathas,*
laid in with layers of mashed potatoes or scraped radishes and
thoroughly fried in pure *ghee.* Excellent stuff, that! And thick
curds. And of course turnip and cauliflower pickles! How one

relishes those *parathas* with curds after a lively round of fun and frolic!'

Khanna Sahib smacked his lips, savouring the delicacies in his imagination. For a while he sat silent, stiffly leaning back in the saddle. 'I pity these hybrid Indians,' he said, continuing his monologue. 'These westernized sophisticates—they are neither Indians nor Europeans! One must have a strong stomach to digest these rich foods. Only a Punjabi can digest the Punjabi food.'

During the British regime Hasandin had seen many Punjabi visitors who lived in European style. 'Sa'b, I know many Punjabis who eat and dress like the white Sahib,' he blurted out.

'As for dress, I'm not averse to wearing European clothes,' Khanna Sahib said. 'But where food is concerned I prefer our own. All this English food, boiled meat and vegetables and dishes without spices and chillies—do you call it food? The English food is utterly insipid, unfit for human consumption. Just think, can roast mutton and cold meat come anywhere close to *korma* and *roghan-josh*? And who would like to have sliced bread when he can have *parathas* saturated in pure *ghee*? To tell the truth, I prefer coat and trousers when I have to go out and do a lot of horseback riding. But down there in Delhi I wear nothing but a *tehmet*. A *kurta* and a *tehmet* are more comfortable any time than a coat and pants. A flowing silk *kurta* on your back, a loose silk *tehmet* round your waist, and a pair of Kamalia country shoes—what more does one want? They're so light and comfortable you want to fly rather than walk. I tell you, the secret of a Punjabi's robust health is his loose garments and abundant good food.'

Hasandin laughed goodhumouredly. 'Yes, Sa'b, you're right. I mean about the Punjabis. A Punjabi knows how to enjoy the good things of life. Just about five years ago a Punjabi used to visit

Gulmarg every season. He stayed at the Nido's. He would send word to me the moment he arrived: "Hasandin, come down with your horse." He preferred my horse to the others. Once I took him to Alpatthar. As it happened, a storm broke over Afrabat. No sledge was available. I spread my oilcloth on the snow and we both sat in it—I in front, and he behind, his arms around my waist. I propelled the cloth and we went sliding merrily down the snowy slope. The Sa'b was pleased. He gave me ten rupees as *bakshish*. You know, he threw about money like the white Sa'bs.'

'Of course, Punjabis are Punjabis!' Khanna Sahib said stabbing the air with his right hand. 'They are generous to a fault. Now take my case...' And he launched forth on a long story illustrating his own generosity: 'Last Sunday I hired a *shikara* for the whole day to have an excursion on Dal Lake. My plan was to do the Shalimar, Nishat Gardens and Chashma Shahi, have a brief stopover at Nehru Park, and end up at Meerankadal, where I had my houseboat. The shikara-wallah demanded thirteen rupees, but he came down to ten. When the trip was over I gave him fifteen rupees instead of ten.'

As Khanna Sahib finished the story his face glowed with a beatific light.

'Sa'b, there was one thing about the Punjabi I was just now talking about: he never bargained.' Hasandin said, carefully guiding the horse through a brook.

Khanna Sahib's face darkened. He sat stiffly in the saddle till the horse had crossed the brook and then said : 'Hasandin, don't forget I am a businessman. I must bargain over every deal, big or small. As the saying goes, even the mother and daughter keep accounts between them. You see, the mother would ask her daughter to account for every single paisa, even if she had a mind to give away a *lakh* of rupees to her.'

Khanna Sahib's face again lit up with joy, as if he had satisfactorily scuttled Hasandin's objection.

Hasandin gave an understanding nod. 'You have put it nicely, Sa'b!'

Khanna Sahib was pleased. To drive the point home, he came out with another story, this time about his grandfather who was said to be a man of a charitable disposition. His business expanded and bit by bit he piled up a huge fortune of over a lakh. But one day in a fit of generosity, he gave away his whole fortune in charity.

The story had whetted Hasandin's curiosity and he was eager to know more about this modern Hatamtai. But suddenly Khanna Sahib's attention was drawn to Kukku's horse, which had broken into a canter. Instead of pulling in the rein, the child was spurring the horse to greater speed. Horrified, Khanna Sahib started shouting frantically. Although Hasandin assured him that there was no danger, Khanna Sahib raced after the child.

NINE

Hasandin stopped the horse at the end of a bazaar. Khanna Sahib dismounted.

'Sa'b, the Rishi's tomb is over there,' he pointed. 'The horses will wait here. Will you have your lunch first, or visit the tomb? Your friends are over there going towards the slope. Perhaps they want to rest for a while.'

'We'll first see the tomb,' Khanna said with staccato brevity.

Unnoticed, Khanna Sahib's son had made a beeline for the nearby shops. When Khanna Sahib and Hasandin caught up with him, he was demanding to be shown a necklace of green stones.

'These necklaces are for girls,' Khanna Sahib said. 'You're not a girl, are you?'

It was a small bazaar consisting of a few nondescript shops, which sold the daily necessities of life—rice, pulses, flour, *schyeru,* bread, green tea, cheap cigarettes and *biris,* matches, caps, cheap cloth and the like. There was nothing of interest for tourists, except stone necklaces and cheap silver trinkets, which were in fact made of nickel.

'Buy him a necklace, Sa'b,' Hasandin pleaded on behalf of the child.

'Do you see his game, Kukku?' Khanna Sahib said, giving out a hollow laugh. 'Hasandin wants to make you a girl.'

By then Kukku had fastened his attention on a conical Kashmiri cap.

Khanna Sahib laughed still louder. 'Syces wear those caps,' he said. 'See, Hasandin is also wearing one. Do you want to be a *hato*?'

Mrs Khanna took hold of Kukku's hand and tried to drag him away. 'Come, we're already late,' she said. 'We'll first have Baba Rishi's *darshan* and then eat something. After that I'll buy you whatever you like.'

The child was adamant. Cajoling the boy and whispering into his ear, Mrs Khanna dragged him away from the shop. Hasandin was surprised at the Sahib's reluctance to part with a paltry eight *annas* for the sake of his child. 'What kind of a Sa'b is he?' he wondered.

Baba Rishi's tomb was a little way beyond the bazaar. They first had to pass through a row of rooms in which the devotees and attendants of the tomb lived. In the open space adjoining the rooms, a big cauldron had been set on a fire around which a group of Kashmiri women was dancing, singing hymns of praise to the great saint. Walking past them, Hasandin led Khanna Sahib to the tomb.

Khanna Sahib lingered outside. 'Its roof is similar to the roof of Shah Hamdan's tomb,' he said explaining the finer points of architecture to his wife.

A coloured curtain hung across the narrow door. As they reached the door, the Mohammedan priest lifted the curtain for them to enter. Inside there was a big rectangular room, the saint's grave resting in the middle. Hasandin bowed in reverence before the grave and Khanna Sahib, his wife and the child, mechanically followed his example. Then they circumambulated the grave. The inner vault was carved in wood, with trellised windows to let in the air.

'Hasandin, why have they tied threads and hair to the trellis work?' Khanna Sahib asked examining the carvings minutely.

Hasandin explained the importance of tying a thread or a hair and said, 'Sa'b, ask for a boon. It'll be granted to you.'

Khanna Sahib took a thread from the priest and his wife plucked a hair from her head. Tying them round the trellis work they silently asked for their respective boons. Khanna Sahib wished for success in securing the military contract on which he had set his heart, and his wife, for the blessing of another child. Kukku was now ten years old and she had not conceived since.

They again bowed before the grave, made another circumambulation, and filed out of the tomb. The Mohammedan priest looked at them hopefully.

'Sa'b, you must offer some money,' Hasandin said. 'It's the custom.'

Khanna Sahib felt his pockets. 'I don't have any change,' he said to the priest. 'Only ten rupee notes. We'll come some other time and make proper amends. If our wishes are granted, we'll make a handsome offering.' He was not familiar with any language but the one of give-and-take, which smacked of bribery.

The priest laughed and blessed them. Khanna Sahib explained to his wife in English that he was not such a fool as to make any offering before his boon was granted. As he walked out, he laughed self-complacently.

Hasandin was disturbed at Khanna Sahib's failure to make an offering at the tomb. 'May I offer a rupee or two on your behalf?' he was on the verge of saying, when he suddenly stopped himself, lest the Sahib take offence. Instead, he took two *annas* from his pocket and put them on the threshhold. Bowing before the shrine he then ran out to join the others.

When they reached the bazaar, Khanna Sahib suggested they settle down somewhere to eat and then rest for a while. In the meantime Hasandin could have his tea and meet them after two hours. And he picked up the canvas bag.

'I'll carry it, Sa'b.' Hasandin said taking away the bag from him.

'Where's the spring? We would like to stop somewhere near the water.'

'Don't worry about the water, Sa'b. I'll fetch it for you. There's a nice place over there,' Hasandin said and then hesitated for a second. 'If you don't mind, Sa'b, may I ask for some money. I've to buy food for the boys.'

Khanna Sahib shoved his hand into his pocket and brought out a ten rupee note. 'I forgot to get change. You see, I've also run into debt to Baba Rishi.' And he laughed.

Hasandin looked at the note. 'Couldn't you give me some things smaller? Say a rupee? I could manage with that for now.'

Khanna Sahib laughed again, 'A pity I forgot to carry change.' He paused. 'How about getting the note cashed?'

'Who'll change a ten rupee note in this place?' Hasandin said gloomily.

'Then take the note!' Khanna Sahib said dramatically, holding out the note before Hasandin. 'Surely, I owe you a lot of money.'

Hasandin was hoping that Khanna Sahib would engage his horses the following day to go to Khilanmarg and did not want to prejudice his chances.

'Keep the note, Sa'b,' he said, 'I'll manage somehow.'

Khanna Sahib promptly put the note back into his pocket and said expansively, 'Yes, yes, you pay from your pocket, we'll settle accounts later.' Hasandin ran up to Mamdoo and giving him eight *annas*, told him to get something to eat for himself and Idu. The Sahib had not given any tip as yet, he said. He'll return as soon as he'd settled the Sahib and his party.

When Hasandin returned, he found Khanna Sahib waiting for him. His wife, standing a little apart, was waiting for them both. Kukku had run up to see Prof Uppal, who was sitting a little further up with his party.

Khanna Sahib moved up the hill in leisurely strides, his wife following him, as if looking for a decent spot to settle down for lunch. 'Papoji, come here!' his son shouted.

'No, Kukku, you come here. We'll sit somewhere here,' Khanna Sahib shouted back, feigning anger.

But the boy refused to budge from his palce. Then, Prof Uppal chipped in, 'Come over, sir, come and join us.'

Khanna Sahib sauntered over with reluctant steps. Tins of jam and butter lay open before them. Prof Uppal's niece was making sandwiches and they were all busy eating, including Khanna Sahib's son, who was freely partaking of the sandwiches.

'Please sit down and help yourself.' Prof Uppal said making room for Khanna Sahib and holding out the plate of sandwiches.

'Thanks a lot. But we have brought *parathas.*'

'Eat *parathas* by all means,' Prof Uppal said, 'but have some of these, too. My stomach is not too good. Otherwise I relish *parathas*. Usha will keep you company.'

With that he spread some jam on a slice of bread, took a large bite and munched contentedly.

Khanna Sahib took the canvas bag from Hasandin and brought out a tin box. Opening it he offered a *paratha* to each of those present.

Usha curled up her nose at the sight of the stale *parathas* and Prof Uppal had to warn her quietly not to forget her manners. Taking the hint, the young man from Africa bit off a piece, munched it slowly, and declared that it tasted nice.

'*Parathas* go well with curd and turnip pickle.' Khanna Sahib said cheerfully. 'These *parathas* have become a little cold. But when they come sizzling straight from the frying pan—ah, how nice they taste! You risk chewing up your fingers along with them'

Inviting Usha and the young man from Africa to have some more *parathas,* Khanna Sahib unashamedly helped himself to the sandwiches.

Hasandin was watching all this from a distance. When Khanna Sahib emptied the tin, he handed it to Hasandin to clean it and to fetch some water from the spring. Mrs Khanna said that she would bring the water herself.

'You don't bother,' Khanna Sahib said. 'Let him bring the water.'

When Hasandin came with the water, Kukku snatched the tin away from him. Mrs Khanna got up on the pretext of seeing the spring. She drank some water from the spring and then rinsed her mouth.

When Kukku had finished drinking, Khanna Sahib took the tin from him and quaffed the remaining water in one large swallow. He had stuffed himself with more food than he could cope with. He belched loudly and reclined languidly on the grass.

'It's time you visited the tomb,' he said lazily to Prof Uppal, trying to make small talk.

'Oh, I've no faith in these saints,' Prof Uppal said. 'Usha was keen on visiting the tomb, and Jivanand,' he pointed towards the young man, 'also wanted to have a look, so they dragged me along, too. I was feeling hungry and homage to the stomach took precedence over homage to the saint.'

Khanna Sahib laughed. But Hasandin covered his ears with his hands, considering it a sacrilege to hear the saint being disparaged.

'What's your plan for tomorrow?' Khanna Sahib asked.

Hasandin perked up his ears.

'Usha wants to go to Khilanmarg. But I'm not joining the game. I'd like to rest.'

'We ourselves are thinking of going to Khilanmarg. Why don't you come along, too? We could take the frozen lake and Alpatthar also in our stride.'

'Uncle, do come along!' Kukku clung to Prof Uppal's neck. Prof Uppal gathered the pretty child in his arms.

'Yes, do come, uncle.' Usha urged. 'If the exertion proves too much for you, you can relax on the bank of Donala, while we'll run upto the lake.'

'Uncle, when you get tired you can lean on my arm,' Kukku said hanging on Prof Uppal's neck. Uppal kissed him on the cheek. 'All right, son, I'll go with you.'

'God is great!' Hasandin bowed his head in prayer. Wishing to grant his prayer, God had made the child the instrument of its fulfilment.

TEN

When they had finished eating, Prof Uppal stretched himself on the ground. Khanna Sahib lay sprawled on the edge of Prof Uppal's *durrie,* his stomach working overtime to digest the food. His wife had left to buy a cap for Kukku. Hasandin enthusiastically set out to make another trip to the saint's tomb with Usha and Jivanand. His heart was filled with reverence for Baba Rishi who according to the popular belief had become one with God, and Hasandin regarded it as an act of great piety to take visitors for the saint's *darshan.*

He narrated with gusto the miracles attributed to the saint and explained the significance of the big cauldron in which a fat sheep was being cooked. He also showed Usha and Jivanand the relics of the saint, and suggested that they tie a thread round the trellised window and ask for a boon.

Jivanand was a tall, slim, wheat complexioned and sharp-featured, young man. He was listening Hasandin in a dreamy haze without asking any questions. Usha, on the other hand, kept up a continuous patter, probing Hasandin for more information; and Hasandin, on his part, replied to her queries with great diligence as if it were a solemn ritual. When Hasandin suggested that Jivanand may tie a thread on the trellised window, the young man started looking into space as if Hasandin were addressing someone else. As Usha looked at Jivanand her eyes lit up, a flush rose to her cheeks and her lips trembled.

'I'll ask for a boon,' she said glancing meaningfully at Jivanand. But there was a faraway look in Jivanand's eyes as if his gaze had travelled to the unknown jungles of Africa. Usha simmered with excitement and a strange glow pervaded her face.

A young woman of medium height, not exactly fat but with a marked tendency towards plumpness, Usha mentioned her age was twenty-one, but looked thirty. At first she would strike as the housewifely type, mother of at least one child. Like any educated woman, she dressed with meticulous care, and yet she betrayed faint signs of grossness. In other words, refinement was not her strong point. As she stood inside the tomb, eyes half-closed, her face had become animated, like a dark room suddenly brightened by a ray filtering through a hidden casement.

'Where can I get a piece of thread?' she suddenly asked Hasandin.

'Why, you can pull out from your plait-strings as the Kashmiri women do,' Hasandin wanted to tell her. But instead, he hurried to the priest and promptly returned with a piece of thread.

Usha cast a furtive glance at Jivanand and, tying the thread round the trellised window, silently asked for a boon. Her eyes were closed, her face mellow with tenderness, like the twilight glow of evening rippling over the parched earth. Her lips trembled in prayer. Opening her eyes, she looked at the youth—tall, slim and reticent. His gaze had returned from the dark, dense jungles of Africa. Their eyes met. A faint aura of rapture rippled across her face. The youth's expression took on a gloomier tone. They turned back in silence.

Hasandin did not see this tender drama. Eyes closed and head bowed, he thanked the saint for having heard his humble servant's prayers and giving him such good customers. He renewed his vow to the saint that, as soon as he had some money, he would perform Idu's marriage in deference to his mother's wishes, and bring the couple to the tomb to ask for the saint's benediction. The only hitch was lack of money, and he prayed for help in that respect. He also prayed that the Baba grant the young lady's wishes so that they may come again to Gulmarg and he may bring them here.

When he opened his eyes, Usha and Jivanand had reached the door of the vault. Hasandin hastened after them. Usha bowed at the threshold.

'*Huzoor*, its customary to give something in charity for the poor,' Hasandin said.

Usha looked about helplessly. She had left her purse with her uncle. Noting her embarrassment, Jivanand immediately fished out a few one rupee notes from his pocket and laid them at the edge of the grave. Hasandin was pleased. The sacrilege that Khanna Sahib had committed in not making an offering to the saint had been atoned.

When they came out, Jivanand held out a one rupee note to Hasandin. 'This is for your tea.'

'No, Sa'b,' Hasandin said, overwhelmed. 'I'll not accept anything for showing you round the tomb. It's an act of piety. When you hire my horse and you are satisfied with my work, I won't hesitate to ask for a *bakshish*.'

Hasandin returned to the bazaar in high spirits. He ate *schyeroos* and drank the salted green tea. Then he hurried back to Khanna Sahib.

They came down by a different route so that they could have a view of the hills at the other end of Gulmarg. Hasandin brought them to the exact spot, where they had made a brief halt before reaching Gulmarg. Their hotel was clearly visible.

'Papoji, we have reached our hotel!' Kukku said excitedly.

Khanna Sahib took the canvas bag from Hasandin. 'How much?' He brought out his purse.

'Payment can wait, Sa'b. Aren't you going to Khilanmarg and Alpatthar tomorrow? I'll take you there. I'll take the money then.'

'I've a mind to visit Khilanmarg,' Khanna Sahib said. 'But I'm not sure about Alpatthar. You see, I've already booked our seats on tomorrow's bus. I don't want to miss the bus. It'll mean a loss of another eight or ten rupees. That's a big amount!'

'You needn't worry, Sa'b. If you start early enough, you can easily make the trip to Alpatthar and the frozen lake and return in time to catch the bus.'

'What time should we start?'

'Say about seven in the morning. We can reach Afrabat by about eleven. Better sleep early so you can be ready by six.'

'What time will you show up?'

'I'll be here at six-thirty.'

'I don't have an alarm clock. Better come at six to wake us up and to see that the bearer gets our food ready.'

'You need have no worry, Sa'b. I'll be here at six.'

'All we require is a dozen *parathas* and a vegetable without gravy. As for pickles, we have plenty with us.'

'Sa'b, also order a few omelettes. It's cold up there. Eggs will keep you warm.'

'We don't eat eggs!'

'Don't worry, Sa'b. I'll convey your instructions to the bearer. Will you have your morning tea in bed?'

'Only those who ape the Englishmen take bed-tea,' Khanna Sahib said, laughing mirthlessly. 'I take a glass of cold water in the morning. I'm not in the habit of taking bed-tea.'

Hasandin made a move towards the hotel. 'And listen,' Khanna Sahib said. 'Tell the bearer not to prepare *parathas* just now. He must make them in the morning so that they remain fresh.'

'Don't worry, Sa'b.' Coiling the blanket around his neck Hasandin turned and said, 'Your instructions will be carried out to the letter.'

It was not yet six, but darkness had descended over Gulmarg. The rows of shops in the small bazaar, shrouded in mist, had lost their contours. A few lights had come on. To the right, the snow-capped peak of Afrabat had lost its lustre. The cold had increased.

Mrs Khanna took the bag from her husband. 'How about a stroll in the bazaar?' Khanna Sahib said.

'Do you call it a bazaar?' She replied. 'I'm told only the *dhaba* is open. All the other shops have closed, even the government emporium. What's there to see?'

'Just a brief stroll.'

'Aren't you tired of roaming? My whole body is aching.'

Hasandin returned after giving necessary instructions to the bearer. 'Sa'b, you must rest now. Tomorrow I'll take you through the bazaar.' He salaamed Khanna Sahib and then his wife.

'What about me?' Kukku said. 'Don't you know I'm the Burra Sahib?'

Amused, Hasandin gave a low bow. 'Burra Sahib, salaam!' He said with a smile.

He came out on to the road. Idu and Mamdoo were sitting by the side, smoking *biris*. Beckoning them to get up, he put his foot in the stirrup and was astride the horse in one leap.

'Ya, *Pir!*' he shouted exultantly.

'*Dastgir!*' Idu and Mamdoo shouted in unison as they mounted their horses.

The horses galloped off towards Tangmarg.

ELEVEN

The sun was struggling to peek from behind the eastern range of the mountains when Hasandin, Idu and Mamdoo came racing to Gulmarg.

Last night on reaching home he had fed the horses and then, tying together their forelegs, let them loose on the slope where grass grew in luxurious abundance. The horses hopping on their hindlegs would go far out of the village, but at the break of dawn the villagers would lead them back. Hasandin's horses had been out on duty since early morning. Reaching the pasture they lay on their backs, kicked up their legs and started rolling on the grass.

Whenever he saw them sprawled on the grass, a jingle echoed in Hasadin's mind:

> Why did the water go bad?
> Why did the pot get rusty?
> Why did the horse stop?

And the answer would flash through his mind:

> Because it had not been rolled!

It is strange that a tired man wants to sleep, while a tired horse wants to roll on the ground. Hasandin often thought that if he ever came into a lot of money he would engage a stable boy to tend his horses and give them a good brush up. Many years ago he had seen a syce grooming a white sahib's pony and the scene had got imprinted on his mind.

While returning from the field, thinking of the white sahib's stable made him lapse into his old daydream. This time the police did not get scent of his treasure trove and he found himself richer by a lakh of rupees. It was a staggering amount. The first thing he did was to have some nice clothes made and buy rich food. He bought expensive clothes not only for his wife and children but also for his elder brother's family. His barn was filled to bursting with all kinds of grain. Then he made a new house on the outskirts of his village. This done, he went to keep his vow to Baba Rishi and had Idu married to his elder brother's daughter. Next he had a big stable made for his horses, who then plied between Srinagar, Pehalgam and Gulmarg. The horses were fed on the best of victuals and the syces groomed them with soft cloth pads, the same way as he had seen the white sahib's stable-boy grooming the pony. Money poured, he took a new wife lived with her in a bungalow at Tangmarg.

Just then he heard Yasman, his wife, ask Mamdoo to go and find out if her husband was gossiping at Rehman the grocer's shop. She was telling Mamdoo to remind Hasandin that they were to leave early in the morning; he should finish dinner in time and sleep. Hasandin's reverie snapped. He thanked God that he was not rich and that he had been spared the temptations that flesh is heir to. He wondered how he could ever think of another woman, when

Yasman managed the house so beautifully and was such a self-denying, devoted wife.

With a jerk of his head, he tried to whisk away these unseemly thoughts, and, as he climbed the steps of his decrepit hut, he resolved that if fortune ever smiled on him, he would buy a lot of fine clothes and jewellery for his wife.

While having his food, he told Yasman that God had been kind to him and so he had managed to get good customers in the morning. He had also learned that Harnam Singh was likely to be on morning duty throughout the month. It was such a stroke of good fortune that he could not help passing on the news to his brother, optimistic that in course of time he would be able to save enough money for Idu's marriage.

When he lay down in bed, his wife came and sat near him and they kept awake a long time talking about Idu's marriage and planning a feast in Baba Rishi's honour.

Sprawled in the saucer-like valley, Gulmarg was still drowsy with sleep. In the morning haze the velvety grass had taken on the colour of kidney beans. The Gulmarg nullah stretched across the meadow like a sleepy python. And the goat paths lazily meandering through as if in a trance, were lost in the grass. The Khalsa Hotel and beyond it to the right, the row of shops, uniformly alike, still dozed in the enveloping silence. To the left, below Afrabat, the silver-streaked streams of Donala lay as languidly as slender maidens whose eyes had not known the satiation of love.

But Hasandin had no time to linger over the glory of this morning. Racing his horse across the ridge, he slowed down near the slope, got down from his horse at the gate of the Gulmarg

Hotel and handed the reins to Idu. Throwing the loose end of his blanket over his shoulder, he hurried through the gate. Waking up the bearer, he reminded him that it was time to set about preparing the Sahib's breakfast and packing the lunch.

Since the number visitors had dwindled to a trickle, the hotel owner managed with a bearer and a cook. The bearer's duties included renting out rooms, preparing bills and receiving payments. No one knew whether he was a professional bearer, a poor relation of the hotel owner, or just one of his trusted minions.

'The occupants of Room 3 have to make a trip to Alpatthar this morning and then catch the return bus from Tangmarg,' Hasandin reminded the bearer. 'And the visitor in Room 1 won't leave his bed until he gets tea. His daughter is going to the frozen lake.'

Although Hasandin had rammed these facts into the bearer's head last night, he did not consider it a waste of breath to emphasize them once again. He had assured the two sahibs that he would personally supervise all the details!

In the meantime the cook had got the tea ready, and the bearer hurriedly took it to Uppal Sahib's room. Hasandin woke up Khanna Sahib and asked him to get ready so that his breakfast could be sent up.

Going back to the kitchen, Hasandin told the bearer that he would himself help the cook while the bearer made the sandwiches.

Everything was ready within an hour. The Sahibs seemed to be in no hurry however. Warning them that unless they reached Khilanmarg in time, they would miss the view of the Jhelum and Wular Lake, Hasandin came out to take a few puffs on a *biri*.

Uppal Sahib's syces had already come and were sitting with Idu and Mamdoo, their backs resting against the hotel wall. Hasandin joined them. Fishing out a *biri* from the depths of his *firan* pocket, he lit a match and took a long puff.

The sun had come out, turning the vast field into a mottled pattern of light and shade and imparting a soft glow to the goat paths. Although the slender fields of Afrabat had not been hugged by the warmth of the sun, they had shed their torpor and come alive, imbued with a strange vivacity. It was going on to eight when a call went out for Hasandin.

Hasandin jumped to his feet. Hurriedly throwing the blanket over his shoulder, he went running inside. Khanna Sahib was ready and so was Uppal Sahib. He called Uppal Sahib's syce.

'Here, pick up these things and let's start.' Khanna Sahib said.

It was the same old canvas bag, two raincoats and an umbrella. There were also two walking sticks, which Khanna Sahib had decided to carry with him at the insistence of Hasandin.

'Have you got your lunch packet, Sa'b?' Hasandin asked.

'Yes, I've had *parathas* made. Twelve in all. Dry curry of potatoes and cauliflower. And Wadhawa Singh's turnip pickles. You must have heard of Wadhawa Singh's pickles. They are famous all over India.'

Hasandin tied the canvas bag in his blanket and slung it across his waist. He gave the umbrella and raincoats to Mamdoo and one walking stick to Idu. The other stick he kept with him and helped the visitors mount their horses.

'Where are you going?' Uppal Sahib said, 'Doesn't our route lie the other way?'

'Sa'b, you go by the other route.' Hasandin said. 'My sa'b wants to make a round of the bazaar.'

'I hope we'll get water up there,' Khanna Sahib said.

'Plenty of it, Sa'b. But you'll have to melt the snow. You won't get pure water until you reach Afrabat.'

'What does one do if he feels thirsty?'

'Sa'b, one feels very thirsty while climbing up.' Hasandin paused and then brightened. 'Why not buy a bottle of lemon squash? The English tourists always kept a bottle handy. Ice water is bad for the throat.'

'Ice water may be bad for delicate English throats, but not for ours,' Khanna Sahib laughed. 'Let's buy some lemon drops. We'll suck them when thirsty.'

'That's a good idea, Sa'b,' Hasandin said. 'You can buy as much as you like from this shop here.'

Khanna Sahib laughed. 'I'm not going into business that I need to buy any quantity,' he said. 'A few will do. Buy four *annas*' worth.'

'What do you need so many lemon drops for?' Mrs Khanna chimed in. 'They're awfully sticky and they'll spoil your pockets. Buy two *annas*' worth.'

It was a small wayside shop selling flour, rice, *dal*, *ghee*, vegetables and other necessities. Sitting on the horse, Khanna Sahib handed down a one rupee note. 'Buy four *annas*... no, two *annas*' worth of lemon drops,' he said.

The shopkeeper counted out fourteen *annas* in small change and then placed one lemon drop on Hasandin's outstretched palm.

'Only one lemon drop for two *annas*!' Khanna Sahib said, amazed. 'At our place they sell for one pice each.'

The shopkeeper was a Kashmiri. Probably he did not belong to the trader class and was a Brahmin by caste. Bad times had made him set up a grocer's shop. He was wearing a dirty *firan* and a small soiled turban over his head. His face was wrinkled and his back was stooped. The fair complexion and sharp nose betrayed his Kashmiri origin. He laughed at Khanna Sahib's remark. 'You're lucky that these things are even available here. Don't you realize how distant this place is from the city, where they sell these drops at a pice each?'

Khanna Sahib had no answer to this and gave a hollow laugh to cover up his discomfiture. 'Perhaps you're right,' he said as if warmly commending the shopkeeper. 'Well, make it a *chattack* then,' he said expansively.

While the shopkeeper was weighing the lemon drops in a rusty scale intended only for weighing vegetables and the like, Hasandin's eyes came to rest on the bottles of lemon squash. 'What have the times come to!' he said to himself, 'and what visitors!'

Crossing the green meadow which lay drenched in sunshine, they passed by Nido's Hotel. 'Didn't the frontier tribesmen ransack the hotel?' Khanna Sahib asked.

'They made a thorough job of it, Sa'b,' Hasandin said. 'They carried away everything they could lay their hands on. They even removed the carpets and tore off the electric fittings. They thought it was gold.' Hasandin laughed at their foolishness. 'They thought everything that glittered was gold.'

'Were there no visitors at that time?'

'It was winter time. The season had just ended. The hotel and the bazaar had closed down.'

'I'm told that even the local people joined in the loot.'

'Well, Sa'b, it takes all kinds to make the world.'

The terse manner, in which Hasandin answered, did not encourage Khanna Sahib to ask any further questions.

Hasandin suddenly recalled that distant morning when the frontier tribesmen, intoxicated with victory swept everything before them. They had come to Tangmarg in trucks and after ransacking

it, had pushed on to Gulmarg. They had forced the local people
to go with them and for three days they were made to carry loads
on their backs. One horse was made to do the work of three. They
commandeered a large number of coolies. Not only that, they
carried a lot of things on their own heads. When they were gone,
the villagers took their turn, pillaging what was left. They even
entered into houses, where previously they had not dared step on
the verandahs. They ransacked the drawing rooms, bed rooms and
dining rooms. They made a clean sweep of everything looting all
that remained after the plunder by the tribesmen. In the all round
confusion they also took the opportunity to settle old scores; many
shops were burnt down.

'Ya Pir!' Hasandin said as if whisking away the nightmarish scene
from before his eyes. He sighed deeply.

'Well, Hasandin, what was here before the Britishers came—a
village?'

'No, Sa'b, it was all a jungle. And where you now have the polo
ground, it was nothing but a big marsh.'

'A marsh?'

'Yes, Sa'b. I've not seen it myself, but my grandfather said that
the *nullah* flowed through the polo ground making the whole place
a big marsh. Shepherds grazed their sheep here.'

'Did nobody live here before the Britishers came?'

'My Grandfather said that sometimes Sultan Yusuf Shah visited
this place. But it was actually the Britishers who made Gulmarg
what it is.'

Hasandin conjured up the vision of that first Gulmarg, based on
his grandfather's account. The place was in its primaeval glory and
the meadow of Gulmarg was hedged round by poplars interspersed
with pines, maple and spruce. There were no hotels, no houses, no

huts; neither roads nor bazaars. There were only narrow goat paths, which meandered through the grass and got lost in thick forests. Silence reigned. The whine of the winds and the rustling of trees were the only sounds breaking the stillness. Sometimes the cooing of a hornbill or the song of a solitary shepherd would come trilling over the air and fill the forest.... And then human ingenuity got down to work. Gradually the jungles were cleared, the *nullahs* harnessed and golf links and polo grounds created, and Gulmarg, the dream of the British rulers, became a reality. It was the pride of all hill resorts, the haven of government officials and British gentry.

The climb had begun. Hasandin let go of the reins and, falling behind the horse, slowly trudged his way up. 'Var! var!' he would warn the horse to slow down. There was a party ahead of them— three persons and a horse. Maybe they took turns riding the horse. It occurred to Khanna Sahib that he should have also followed their example. If they could do it why not his family and he?

'We should have taken a horse for Kukku and walked on foot ourselves,' he said to his wife. 'It would have been such fun!'

'You could have no doubt made it on foot.' Hasandin broke in, 'but you wouldn't have been able to return in time. You have a return ticket, don't you?'

Khanna Sahib was silenced. Hasandin again took up the threads of his thoughts....Those were the days! These skimpy types dare not set foot in Kashmir. The Britishers were generous with money. People could find work not only during the four months while the season lasted but even in winter when the mountains were covered with snow. Those fond of skiing flocked to the place. They would start from Afrabat and come toboggaging half way down to Srinagar. The White ruler had many plans for developing Gulmarg. They wanted to lay out a golf course and have a bridle path girdling the hill station where they could go horseriding. They also planned to develop a fishery in the lake for anglers. In short they wanted to make Gulmarg a paradise for everyone, from children to old men. Many of their dreams were realized, many more remained. And then came Independence. They felt Kashmir would soon slip out of their hands. Unwilling to part with Kashmir, they let loose the wolves from across the frontier who ravaged the fair valley in a matter of hours and laid everything waste. Those shops at Gulmarg, which had remained intact, crumbled in the snowfall. In the past there were arrangements to clear the snow and save the houses from getting snowed under. Now such arrangements were completely lacking. The snow would be there throughout the winter and would slowly corrode the roofs.

Now that the tourist traffic had resumed after a lapse of many years, the valley had regained some of its lost glory, but Gulmarg was still sad and forlorn like a bride bereft of her charms. The government had indeed set up two shops, and the hotel owners had sent down a clerk and a few bearers. But one swallow does not make the summer. Previously, the visitors stayed on for months. Now they did not stay beyond a week.

But Gulmarg was gradually coming into its own, thank God. There was a small trickle of tourists. If things continued to improve at this pace and the tourist traffic picked up, the few shops that remained would grow into a bazaar and the shops that were razed would be rehabilitated. The hotels would pick up business, the cottages and bungalows would be tenanted, and the club revived. Gulmarg would again thrive, providing livelihood for the village around. As he walked behind the horse, Hasandin prayed that there would be no more pillage, so that more visitors might come, and stay longer, and that Gulmarg might again become lively and gay.

'What are those tents over there?' Khanna Sahib asked breaking Hasandin's chain of thought.

'That's Khilanmarg, Sa'b,' Hasandin said, sidling forward. 'We'll be there within half an hour.' Breaking a small poplar twig, he swished it against the back of the horse. The horse doubled its pace.

TWELVE

Uppal Sahib, his dumpling of a niece, and the young man from Africa had already reached the next halt and were sitting in camp chairs outside the tent which housed an itinerant Sikh's restaurant.

'Sardarji, get some tea for the Sa'bs,' Hasandin said, going over to the Sikh.

'Badshaho, tea'll be ready in a minute.' The Sikh gave a pleasant smile and put some more coals in the charcoal burner. Picking up the empty tea cup in front of Uppal Sahib, he went away to wash it.

Khilanmarg is at a height of 1500 feet above Gulmarg, and the way to it is rugged and uneven. Khanna Sahib was tired from the day before, and his limbs ached. Getting down from the horse, he yawned deeply and then, taking his wife and child with him, walked towards the restaurant.

'So we meet again!' Uppal Sahib greeted him. 'This trip has taken the wind out of me. And imagine, these people are thinking of going to Afrabat.' He looked indulgingly at Usha and Jivanand and laughed.

'I, too, am in no better shape,' Khanna Sahib grimaced. 'But we propose going as far as Donala, if not Afrabat. I would like to feel the crunch of snow under my feet.'

'Papoji, we must go further upto that peak. You must take my photograph there,' Kukku insisted.

'No child, it'll be to tiring for you,' Khanna Sahib said. 'As for me, I could go upto Afrabat or even to Alpatthar and the frozen lake.'

'No, Papoji. I'll also go upto Alpatthar. I promise I won't get tired.' Getting up from his seat, Kukku clung to his father.

'Don't be impatient, child. We'll go there,' Mrs Khanna said, pulling Kukku away. Then she turned to the Sikh restaurant owner, 'Sardarji, have you anything to eat?'

'I have plenty of things, sister. Biscuits, buns, toast. What will you have?'

'Give him two pieces of toast.'

'No, Mummoji, I'll have a cream roll.'

'They don't have cream rolls over here, silly.' Mrs Khanna said.

'But I must have a cream roll,' Kukku insisted.

'I'll get you one, child, just wait.' The Sikh went inside the tent and came out holding a cream roll in his hand. The pastry looked crisp and tempting.

The child had stretched out his hand to take the pastry when Mrs Khanna pushed away his hand. 'How much?' she fired the question at Sardarji.

'Six *annas!*'

'Six *annas* for this stale piece of cream roll! In Srinagar they sell at three *annas* a piece.'

'It was brought from Srinagar last night. It's absolutely fresh.'

'How do you mean fresh? It is only nine-thirty. How could it arrive from Srinagar so early?'

'It's nearing ten now. My brother brought the pastry just now.

Without replying to the Sikh, Mrs Khanna turned to the child. 'Kukku darling, you shouldn't eat stale pastry. It will upset your stomach. Better have a piece of toast.'

The Sikh thought it futile to argue with Mrs Khanna. He went inside the tent to put the cream roll away.

'Is the tea ready, Sardarji?' Khanna Sahib shouted from his seat.

'It will be ready in a minute *badshaho!* My charcoal burner had gone out. I had to start it again.' The Sikh started fanning the charcoal burner. 'Oh, what terrible cold,' he grumbled. 'I had just got the burner going and had hardly heated a kettle when the charcoals again went out.'

Kukku was still whimpering for the cream roll. 'Come, I'll show you Wular Lake,' Hasandin said.

The child got up with alacrity. Khanna Sahib also rose. 'Uppal Sahib, have you seen the Wular Lake?' he asked.

'No. The mist has blotted out the view. We should have come two hours earlier.'

Hasandin asked the Khannas to follow him. 'Sa'b, come with me. I'll show you the lake.'

Khilanmarg is very rocky, devoid of trees or bushes. The place has only patches of grass where the sheep graze. The patch of grass where the Sikh had pitched his tent was not very big. Hasandin took them to the edge of this small field.

'Now look in the distance. There is the Wular and Jhelum.' Hasandin said.

Khanna Sahib, his wife and child strained their eyes, but could see neither a river nor a lake. If the sky is clear, Khilanmarg commands a view of Gulmarg and beyond it to the valley of Kashmir and to jungles, streams, paddy fields, Wular Lake and the snow-covered peaks of Harmukh and Nanga Parvat. But the sun had come up and a thin haze had descended over the landscape. Although one could see jungles, paddy fields, and streams in the near distance, Wular Lake and the peaks of Harmukh and Nanga-Parvat had disappeared behind the mist.

'Mummoji, where's the Wular Lake?' Kukku asked clinging to his mother.

'I can't see it anywhere.' Mrs Khanna replied slightly peeved.

'Me'm Sahib, look in the direction of my finger,' Hasandin pointed towards a far off range of mountains, 'where you see two peaks like the humps of a camel.'

'Oh yes. I can see it now,' Khanna Sahib said cheerfully. He turned to his wife. 'Do you see that peak resembling the letter M?'

'M? What M?'

'Don't you know the letter M? It's part of the English alphabet. Look in front of you—at the peak shaped like an M between two mountains.'

'Oh yes!'

'The depression that you see between the mountains is actually Wular Lake,' Hasandin said. 'And that thin line on the other side—that's the river Jhelum.'

'I see it. Yes, I can see it!' Khanna Sahib said with exaggerated cheerfulness, although it was apparent from his tone that he lacked conviction.

'See what?' Mrs Khanna said testily. 'I can't see anything. And this fellow said that we'd have a very clear view of the lake from

Khilanmarg. These people lure the innocent tourists by giving them false hopes. I know their tricks.'

'Mem Sa'b, I swear by Bapam Rishi,' Hasandin said. 'I never make a false promise. The Sikh hotel owner will tell you that one can have a magnificent view of the lake if one comes early enough. That's why I wanted you to start early. I was at the hotel at six. If you had started in time the mist and the clouds would not be there. Now look! You can still see the peaks of Harmukh and Nanga Parvat. You can get a glimpse of them through the clouds.'

Khanna Sahib looked towards the mountains. It was not easy to distinguish the two peaks from the array of white clouds that surrounded them, but he said gaily that he could see them.

'Sa'b, you'll have a clearer view from Afrabat,' Hasandin said. 'I'll show you everything. First you finish you tea. If you want to catch the bus, you must be up at Afrabat by one o'clock the latest.'

Mrs Khanna and the child were trying unsuccessfully to see the peaks when the Sikh restaurant owner came and said that their tea was ready.

THIRTEEN

'We've fixed up everything,' Uppal Sahib said pushing his chair towards Khanna Sahib. 'Jivanand and Usha will go with you upto the frozen lake. I'll wait for you at Donala.' And he spilled out a mouthful of the choicest epithets as a tribute to the gout, which kept him from going up.

'I want to turn back from Donala myself. But the child wants me to show him the frozen lake.'

The Sikh restaurant owner placed cups of tea in front of them and was about to offer toast to the child when Khanna Sahib saw that Hasandin was standing by their table.

Khanna Sahib sensed that Hasandin was going to make a request. 'Yes, Hasandin, what's the matter?' He asked.

'*Huzoor*, may I have some money for tea?'

'What will you do with money? Have a cup each on my account.'

'No, *huzoor*, we'll have tea in the tent.'

Khanna Sahib turned and saw a small dirty tent pitched behind the restaurant. A few coolies and syces were sitting there drinking tea.

'You must take your tea with us,' Khanna Sahib insisted. He ordered the hotel owner to bring them a cup each.

'But these people will not drink my tea,' the Sikh said apologetically.

'You bring the tea. I'll make them drink it.'

The Sikh shrugged his shoulders and went away.

Hasandin stepped forward and said in a firm tone, 'No, Sa'b, we won't drink his tea. Better you give us some money.'

'I won't give you any money.' Khanna Sahib said. 'Do you want tea or do you want to play games with me.'

'Sa'b, I've told you, we don't drink this tea. We buy it in our tent.'

'If you want tea, drink it with us. Otherwise buy it with your own money.'

'Then give me eight *annas*. Put it on my account.'

'Here, take a rupee,' Khanna Sahib said as if in a fit of generosity. He carelessly threw a rupee note in Hasandin's direction and took a sip from his cup.

Picking up the rupee Hasandin went into the tent and asked the Muslim teaseller to prepare some salted tea for the three of them. Kashmiri tea was boiling in a samovar. The teaseller handed Hasandin, Mamdoo and Idu earthen cups and poured out a light pink concoction. The tea was too hot for Hasandin to hold in his hand. He held the cup with the end of his *firan* and sipped the tea slowly. As he drank, it occurred to him that he had seriously erred in sizing up his customers. Decent visitors never annoy their syces. It was common knowledge that Muslims never drank tea prepared by Sikhs. Perhaps it was the result of religious prejudice, based on the fact that Sikhs decapitated their chickens and goats at one stroke while Muslims butchered the animal slowly, reciting the *kalma*. Or perhaps the hate was the slow accretion of the tyranny of the Sikh governors of Kashmir during the reign of Maharaja Ranjit Singh. The communal riots of a few years ago had driven a further wedge between the two communities that inhabited Kashmir. Whatever the reason, Hasandin had seen that decent visitors, whether Englishmen, Hindus or Sikhs, always respected the religious susceptibilities of their syces. It was the usual practice for visitors to give their syces four *annas* at the Khilanmarg halt. The Britishers even gave a rupee each. Obviously Khanna Sahib had played dirty with him to save some money. A man who was so stingy about tea money could not be expected to give *bakshish* to his guides.

Hasandin quickly gulped down the tea in a big mouthful. He did not feel refreshed. 'Give me one more cup,' he said and then added. 'My customer is so niggardly that he won't part with four *annas* even for tea money.'

'I thought he had given you this rupee as *bakshish*.' Mamdoo said.

'Forget about *bakshish*,' Hasandin said. 'We won't go beyond Donala. The *seth* is a fake, a regular phoney!'

The teaseller guffawed. Mamdoo and Idu also laughed, but their laughter was tinged with pathos. The teaseller filled Hasandin's cup from the *samovar*. Hasandin drank in silence. He decided to give no more thought to the matter, but he had hardly taken two sips when the same thought again teased his mind. Small episodes of the past two days, which he had thought too puerile to be noticed, flashed before his mind. In fact, till now he had not been able to understand these Indian visitors. He had seen many *seths* who, to all appearances, looked very simple. They ate only *dal* and *roti*, but gave tips like Englishmen. That was one reason he attached no importance to the fact that Khanna Sahib preferred *parathas* to sandwiches. Now he remembered that although Khanna Sahib had shown great aversion to Uppal Sahib's sandwiches, he had done full justice to them; that he had made no offering at Bapam Rishi's shrine; that he had put him off by showing him a ten rupees note; that he had given him no tea money—these things rankled in Hasandin's mind. He should have seen through the *seth* long ago. He had rarely come across a visitor who managed on lemon drops in place of lemon squash. Well, he should have known better. Perhaps he had been taken in by the way Khanna Sahib had bragged about his grandfather's charitable disposition. Surely, the man was either an utter pauper or a super-miser.

As if this analysis had removed the cobwebs from his mind, Hasandin began sipping his tea leisurely.

Khanna Sahib, his tea finished, was ready to resume the journey. 'Hasandin,' he said coming to the tent, 'let's make a move. We must be at Afrabat by lunch time.'

Quickly gulping down the tea Hasandin rose to his feet, but his mind was not on the job. He would have been happy if Khanna Sahib had called off the rest of the trip at Khilanmarg. But he knew that the tourists who went as far as Khilanmarg invariably made it a point to visit Donala just to have the thrill of walking on the snow. There was no going back for Hasandin, but he decided that, come what may, he would not go beyond Donala. These people might go to Afrabat or Aipatthar, but not he, under any circumstances.

Khanna Sahib's son formed the spearhead of the party. Then came Mrs Khanna followed by Khanna Sahib and Uppal Sahib's party making up the rear. When Usha and Jivanand forged ahead,

Khanna Sahib's boy protested that he wanted to keep the lead. Khanna Sahib pushed him forward, begging Usha and Jivanand to allow the child to walk ahead of them.

The pines and deodars were left far below. The land between Khilanmarg and Donala was rocky with just a little grass and some small bushes. Before them stood the peak of Afrabat from which the glacier flowed down in a broad sweep like a river, splitting into two at Donala. One part flowed down within a mile of Khilanmarg while the other went further down, took a swift turn and disappeared from view.

The party was heading for the stream nearer to Khilanmarg, their eyes fixed on the shimmering snow along the slopes. Hasandin knew that once they reached the snow, these people would stand foolishly around, gaping at it, and then make snowballs and pelt one another. They might even venture to walk a few steps and then start photographing each other. Hasandin wondered why they came all the way from distant places just to indulge in these foolish antics. It made no sense to him—a sheer waste of good money. He had heard that people in the cities used ice to cool their *sherbets*. Then what was the point in covering vast distances and at such huge expenses just to have a look at snow? He prayed to Baba Rishi every day for these people to flock to Kashmir in still larger numbers and go up not only to Donala but also to Afrabat and Alpatthar. He knew the reason why he prayed. He was poor and these people rode his horses and gave him money. But for the life of him, he could not understand why these people came here and squandered money like mad bums on such frivolous pursuits. Hasandin and his friends would sit together and laugh at the quaint ways of these city people. They could understand why the Englishmen visited Kashmir—they came from a cold country and the summer heat of the plains was unbearable for them. They did not come to Kashmir just to touch the snow and go away. They stayed there for months on end, had lots of fun playing on the ice, and went out to hunt bears and musk deer. They didn't just gape at the snow like these city-bred fools.

Hasandin often thought, if he had a lot of money, he would visit Bombay and Calcutta and not hibernate in Kashmir. He would perform his son's marriage, make a proper house for himself, buy a lot of land, where he would plant apple, pear, apricot, walnut and almond trees, and then enter the fruit business and make trips to Delhi, Bombay and Calcutta in connection with his business. He conjured up visions of the gay city life of which he had heard from his friends and wondered what make these people from the plains come to the wilderness of Kashmir, leaving the gaiety of the cities behind.

They were still far from Donala when Khanna Sahib ceremoniously put on his dark glasses. A fellow passenger in the bus had casually remarked that glare was bad for the eyes and that one should not look at the dazzling snow with the naked eyes. The first thing Khanna Sahib did on reaching Kashmir was to buy three pairs of cheap American dark glasses from a Kashmiri optician's shop. Putting on a pair, he also advised his wife and child to do likewise.

Hasandin smiled. How foolish of them! The snow was coated with a thin layer of dust and no longer gave off the sharp glaze that it did in winter. If these people had come here in winter, they would have blindfolded their eyes with black scarves to escape the glare. Then he realized that, being rich, they could afford to throw away money on useless things. The question of whether or not to go to Alpatthar was still hovering on the periphery of his mind when he was suddenly reminded of the tea episode. He felt sure that however rich, Khanna Sahib was none the less tight-fisted. Come what may, he would not go beyond Donala.

At a high point near Donala a big flock of sheep had settled down to rest. Hearing horse-hooves, the sheep scrambled to their feet. One of the sheep crossed over the snow and proceeded to the other side of the glacier. The others followed one by one. Khanna Sahib was enchanted at the sight of the black thin line formed by the sheep along the snowy slope. Dismounting from his horse, he caught hold of Kukku's finger and ran towards the snow. They dug out some snow, made it into snowballs, and pelted each other. Mrs Khanna got down from her horse and sat on a rock. Khanna Sahib threw a snowball at her. She ducked as if it were a ball of burning steel. Then Khanna Sahib took out his camera. Fixing it on the stand, he threw the same black cloth over it and asked his wife and child to sit down on a mound of snow.

They had walked only a few steps when they slipped and fell.

Leaving the camera, Khanna Sahib ran towards them. But before he could reach them, he himself slipped and went sprawling on the snow. They helped one another to their feet, but again slipped and fell.

In the meantime, Uppal Sahib had also arrived and was standing on the edge of the glacier, taking in the view. He could not help laughing as he saw the Khannas falling. Of course, he took care that Khanna Sahib did not hear him. Jivanand merely smiled. Usha guffawed and ran forward to Mrs Khanna's rescue. She had just stepped on the snow when she too slipped and fell. Uppal Sahib laughed out loud.

Leaving the horse in Mamdoo's care, Hasandin had sat down to rest by the edge of the glacier. He had a slight headache. Spreading

out his legs and rolling up the blanket, he put it under his elbow
and leaned back so that he could watch Khanna Sahib fiddling with
his camera. He had never had his photographs taken. Whenever he
saw someone taking a photograph, he would stop to watch like a
fascinated child. Ordinarily had one of his customers fallen on the
snow like this, he would have rushed to the rescue and taught him
how to walk on snow. But today, as he lay there, he was overcome
with a strange lassitude, and felt no urge to get up. As he saw Khanna
Sahib fall, his lips curled in a thin smile. But realizing that it was
unbecoming of him, he wiped the smile off his face. But when Usha
also fell down and when Khanna Sahib slipped again, his innate
sense of duty pricked him. He got up. First he helped Usha to her
feet and escorted her to the edge of Donala. Then he went for the
Khannas, instructing them that the right way to walk on ice was to
dig one's heels in the snow and throw his weight on them.

Coming back to the edge, he sat down and watched Khanna
Sahib taking photographs of his wife and child and then Jivanand
taking snaps of Uppal Sahib and his niece. As Hasandin sat
watching, he recalled the incidents of the past two days. Although
he had brooded over them while covering the distance from
Khilanmarg to Donala, he went over them again. The tea episode
particularly rankled in his mind. It had greatly offended him, more
than any irreverence of Khanna Sahib. Hasandin had indeed come
across visitors who flatly refused to give him tea money, but never
any who had so flagrantly hurt his religious sensibilities. Even Sikh
visitors let him take tea in the Muslim tent. Hasandin was no doubt
a simple man, but, having had to deal with all sorts of tourists for
a long time, he had learned to read their minds. At first he might
have been taken in by Khanna Sahib's outward appearance, his
braggadocio and ready wit, but the tea episode had completely

unmasked him. The man wanted to create an impression of generosity without loosening the purse strings. How brazenly he had waved the ten rupee note before him at the shrine of Baba Rishi and then spared himself by asking him to have tea with them. Hasandin's mind rebelled at the thought. Any urge to do his best for Khanna Sahib and take him to all the places had waned. He had sacrificed two nights' sleep and tired himself out in the hope of good wages and a handsome *bakshish*. But the ache in his limbs now cried for attention like a bottled up feeling, which suddenly erupts from the inmost recesses of the heart. His head had become very heavy and his eyelids drooped. He lay down and fell asleep.

When Khanna Sahib had finished taking his wife's and son's photographs, it was his wife's turn to take some snaps. Jivanand also took Usha's photographs in all sorts of poses. After that Usha took pictures of Jivanand and of her uncle.

Then they decided to push on to Afrabat. Since Uppal Sahib had firmly decided against any more climbing, Usha was all the more insistent on making the trip to Afrabat. At last Uppal Sahib gave permission for her to go with Jivanand and requested Khanna Sahib to take care of her. Before Khanna Sahib could nod his assent, Kukku had caught hold of his new aunt's hand and dragged her towards the horse.

Khanna Sahib called out for Hasandin, who was lying asleep, his body half covered with the blanket. Khanna Sahib shook him. 'Hurry up, Hasandin!' He said.

Hasandin got up rubbing his eyes. His headache had worsened. 'Sa'b, the horses can't go any further,' he said, pressing his temples with his thumb and forefinger. 'The passage is blocked with snow.'

'But you promised to take us as far as we wanted to go.'

'Sa'b, I won't go any further. It's one rupee extra upto Donala. The horses can't go beyond Donala. Most of the visitors turn back from here.'

Khanna Sahib saw a few tourists, two foreigners and a couple of Indians, heading up the hill.

'Gentlemen, how far are you going?' he asked one of the Indian tourists.

'Right now to Afrabat. But if we have time, we'll also visit the frozen lake.'

'Anything special about the frozen lake?'

'How should I know? I've yet to visit it.'

'You see, Sa'b?' Hasandin suddenly said. 'Those people are going on foot. As I said, horses do not go that far.'

Khanna Sahib lost his temper. 'You promised to take us upto Alpatthar, didn't you? Are you trying to be clever with me? What's on your mind? Do you want to leave us midstream? Had I known you wouldn't go any further, I'd have turned back at Khilanmarg.'

Uppal Sahib, Usha and Jivanand, standing a little way up, were eagerly listening to the squabble. Their syces had told them they would not take them beyond Donala. They were waiting for Khanna Sahib to prevail upon Hasandin so that they also could make the whole trip on horseback.

Hasandin made no reply. He heard an inner voice saying, Hasandin! Only this far and no further. You made a mistake. You have selected the wrong customers. Take your money and go away. Upto this point they cannot refuse you payment. The rates are regulated by the government. But if you go further up, you may sweat a lot and yet be paid nothing for your labours.

The pain in his head had increased. He was anxious to get

his money, go back home, take two cups of tea and sleep off his weariness. He would have liked to sleep all of next day.

'All right, I'll call off the trip,' Khanna Sahib barked at him. 'But mind you, I'll not pay you a single *cowrie*. Put up my things.'

Hasandin advanced towards the horses. He knew that he could make Khanna Sahib pay. He'd of course create a lot of fuss, but pay he must. Harnam Singh was on duty. His money was safe.

But Khanna Sahib was a hardboiled egg. He knew all the tricks of the game. 'Take away your horses,' he said. 'We can manage without them. We'll walk.' He snatched his canvas bag from Hasandin and made as if to go.

Uppal Sahib, watching this drama between Khanna Sahib and Hasandin, was deeply amused, but Mrs Khanna was getting worried. She hated to walk. Looking very cross, she stepped forward and said, 'Didn't you promise you'd take us all the way up?'

'Mem Sa'b, I've told you once that the horses can't go to Afrabat.'

'Then let us go as far as they can take us.'

'Mem Sa'b, I've a severe headache. Otherwise who wouldn't care to make some extra money?'

'Wait, I'll give you some balm. Rub it on your forehead.' Mrs Khanna turned to her husband. 'Here, hand me the bag.'

Khanna Sahib, who was just putting on a show, turned back at once and handed the bag to his wife. Mrs Khanna rummaged through it and took out a small container of *Amrutanjan*. 'Apply it to your forehead,' she said, giving the bottle of balm to Hasandin.

While applying the ointment, Hasandin gave the matter a second thought. He would do well to go with Khanna Sahib. Being a syce from the Tangmarg stand, he might not be able to get another customer at Gulmarg for the return trip. His day would be spoiled.

And what guarantee was there that Khanna Sahib would hire his horse at Khilanmarg on the way back? *Bakshish* or no *bakshish*, he must complete the trip. So he compromised on the issue. He would do his best to please his customers and leave the rest to God.

Helping the three of them to mount their horses, he took the canvas bag from Mrs Khanna, slung it across his shoulder, and moved on. Usha and Jivanand also got on their horses. Uppal Sahib was still going to stay behind.

'You see, they're rogues,' Khanna Sahib said in English to his wife and Uppal Sahib, 'I know how to deal with them.'

Hasandin felt as if someone were hammering his head. He tied the blanket round it.

Mrs Khanna was not well educated enough to understand her husband's remark. But she guessed its purport and smiled.

Just then Kukku saw a boy swiftly sliding down from Afrabat in a sledge and coming to a stop near Donala. Others were also following him in sledges.

'Papoji, I'd also like to ride a sledge.' Kukku shouted to his father.

'Of course, son, I'll get you one,' Khanna Sahib said and spurred his horse.

As if waiting for just this moment, a young Kashmiri carrying a sledge on his shoulder appeared from behind a rock and started walking by Khanna Sahib's side.

'Well, what are your charges for a ride from Afrabat,' Khanna Sahib asked the young man.

'Eight rupees.'

'Eight rupees!' Khanna Sahib laughed. He jerked his head and, looking in the other direction, dug his heels in the horse's flanks.

The Kashmiri kept walking by his side.

FOURTEEN

The route beyond Donala was a zigzag path ascending through high rocks. To the right was the snowy slope of Afrabat glacier, which ended at Donala. One could never guess how deep the snow lay. A stream must be flowing somewhere through the gorges. In winter the gorges had filled up with snow, overflowing the edges, and they had not yet started to melt. As they advanced towards Afrabat, the expanse of snow became wider, until it looked almost like a plain at the top. One wondered if there were a similar plain and slope at the other end of the peak. While ascending that zigzag path they would come to the edge of the glacier only to drift away again among the rocks. It was a painfully slow climb.

In fact, there was no defined route to Afrabat, though constant streams of visitors had beaten out a narrow path. Every now and then Hasandin grumbled that his horses might slip and come to grief. The horses always stopped at Donala and never ventured beyond. Had Khanna Sahib told him at Tangmarg that he had definite intentions of visiting Alpatthar, he would have taken him by a different route. Those who took this route always made the journey on foot.

Taking no notice of Hasandin's grumbling, Khanna Sahib was busy settling the rate with the sledgewallah. Within the course of about a mile the man had brought his rate down from eight to four rupees and Khanna Sahib had gone up from one to one and a half rupees. This sledgewallah was the sole competitor for Khanna Sahib's business. The other sledgewallahs kept deliberately away. When the path dipped towards the gorge, they could be seen, sledges on their shoulders, slowly climbing towards Afrabat. Perhaps they were the same men, who had been engaged a short while ago by the tourists at Afrabat.

Several times Kukku had implored his father to let him have a sledge ride. 'Papoji, you will hire a sledge for me, won't you?' he asked again and again. When his father said he could have the sledge, Kukku held the imaginary reins in his left hand and chopped the air with his right as if whizzing past in the sledge. 'Mummoji, will you also ride with me?' he asked. He wanted to be reassured that he would not be denied a sledge ride.

Khanna Sahib did not like his son reminding him again and again about the sledge. It weakened his bargaining position. If the sledgewallah got an inkling that Khanna Sahib could be induced by his son to hire a sledge, he would drive a hard bargain with him. But Khanna Sahib knew his own mind; he was the last man to throw away four rupees on a sledge ride.

'My good man, why are you still after me?' he said turning to the sledgewallah. 'You're only wasting your time. There are other visitors coming behind us. They are rich guys. Try your luck with them. We'd prefer to walk down from Afrabat.'

But the sledgewallah would not give up so easily. 'Sa'b, you are a rich *seth*. What do four rupees matter to you? Don't be so stingy. When you have come all the way to Kashmir from such a distant place, why stint on money? Riding a sledge is mighty fun. You'll find youself in heaven. Believe me, I don't charge a pice less than eight rupee. Just now the other sledgewallahs charged eight rupees from those other passengers.'

'Had I been a rajah,' Khanna Sahib said, 'I would have paid you eighty rupees in place of eight. But as you see, I'm a poor man.'

'How you talk, *seth*. No poor man would visit Kashmir. You have spent thousands. Why do you grudge me a small amount—you, who are such a rich *seth*.'

A rich *seth*, my foot! Hasandin said to himself. He must be a measly shopkeeper, the way he bargains.

Hasandin's head was splitting with pain. While the balm's tingling sensation lasted, he had felt some relief, but as its effect wore off, the pain came on again. He wound the blanket tightly round his head. His nose had started running and he wiped it with the end of his sleeve. Money does not make a man rich, he thought to himself. One must be large hearted.

'Brother, help me to settle the rate with the *seth*,' the sledgewallah said to Hasandin in Kashmiri, falling in step with him.

'The *seth* is a skin-flint—a perfect miser,' Hasandin replied to him in Kashmiri. 'But he has to catch the evening bus from Tangmarg and he also wants to visit Alpatthar. He'll have to hire a sledge if he wants to be in time for the bus. But he won't pay you more than two and a half rupees.'

The sledgewallah came forward again. 'Sa'b, your son is eager to do sledgeriding. For his sake, I will accept three and three quarters. I'll not accept a pice less. Take it or leave it.'

In reply Khanna Sahib dug into the sides of his horse and urged it on.

Hasandin's head was still splitting with pain. He decided to go only upto the snow bridge and no further. Whether Khanna Sahib retained his horses or not, he would not go back on his decision. He wiped his nose with the sleeve of his *firan*.

FIFTEEN

The snow bridge was a mile and a quarter from Donala. Actually it was a misnomer to call it a bridge, for no bridge existed. The place was one huge mass of snow from Afrabat to Donala. But in a month or two, when the snow started melting, its water cut a deep tunnel through the snow, which seemed to bridge the two huge masses on the sides. At the time Khanna Sahib made the trip, there was only a slushy footpath extending from one end to the other. The horses stopped at the near end. Hasandin said that the horses could go no further and asked Khanna Sahib to get down.

'But you said that the horses would go right upto Afrabat,' Khanna Sahib said showing no signs of getting down.

'Sa'b, had you come in August when the route was open, I would have taken you right upto Afrabat on horseback. But now the route is blocked. If the horse slips or breaks its legs, you will go tumbling down to Donala.'

'But I am told horses can walk on snow.'

'Sa'b, the other syces are already objecting to my bringing the horses here. If I defy them they'll excommunicate me. I have told you, I won't go a step further.'

Khanna Sahib was too shrewd to miss the note of firmness in Hasandin's voice. But he still did not get down. Like a stubborn child he insisted, 'But you promised to take me upto Afrabat.' He looked back—Usha and Jivanand had got down from their horses.

'Sa'b, I would not have objected. But what can I do? The route is blocked.' He paused for a while and then said, 'I'm neither worried about my horse, nor about myself. I'm worried about you, your Mem Sa'b and the child. If something happens to them, I'll be blamed. It will bring me a bad name.'

Nor was Khanna Sahib worried about Hasandin and his horses. All he cared was about his wife and the child. He dismounted. The path was so narrow and the slope so steep that it sent a shudder through him. 'How will I walk on this snow?' he said helplessly.

'Leave that to me, Sa'b. I'll take all of you across.'

'You'll have to come with me upto Afrabat.'

'I'm unwell, Sa'b.'

'I'll give you *bakshish*.'

'It's kind of you, Sa'b. I'm your slave. But I have a headache. I can't even stand.'

He handed the reins of the horse to Mamdoo and instructed him to wait at Donala.

Khanna Sahib's son, a bold child, was eager to be the first to cross the passage. Hasandin held his hand and, telling him to walk steadily keeping his weight to the left, led him across the narrow wraithlike path made slushy by the constant passage of tourists. When he successfully got across, the boy jumped and clapped his hands with joy. Mrs Khanna was the second to cross with Hasandin's help.

Khanna Sahib slipped twice and got so scared that he forgot to see the beautiful view around him. When he fell the second time

and Hasandin had steadied him to his feet, his eyes roved over the
slope where far below a thin line of ants was slowly moving forward.
These were the sheep which had crossed over to the other end and
were now coming back to the place from which they had started.
As he looked at the sheep it flashed through Khanna Sahib's mind
that if he slipped and went hurtling down the slope he was sure
to collide against the sheep, hurling many of them to their doom.
Overcome by fear his imagination ran berserk. He imagined that
he had already slipped and was rolling down the slope at terrific
speed. Crashing against the line of sheep, he swept many of them
with him. At last he stopped where the snow had come to an end
and where the stream, released from the snowy tentacles, gently
flowed through its stonebed… Cold sweat broke out on his body
and he felt his vest become damp. Leaning against Hasandin, he
took a few quick steps and went across the passage. Thank God
the ordeal was over.

Hasandin turned back to bring Usha and Jivanand, but he saw
that Jivanand was supporting Usha and they had almost crossed
over.

Khanna Sahib stood still for a few minutes. Afrabat rose sheer above
him. The steep climb and the slow progress over, the snow bridge
had made him breathless, but his son, eagar to move on, tugged at
his mother's arm.

Khanna Sahib was about to follow his wife, when Hasandin
stopped him. 'Sa'b, take this bag,' he said, 'I'm unwell. I'll wait for
you at Donala.'

'But you must accompany us to Afrabat,' Khanna Sahib snapped.
'It's because of you that we have come here.'

'Sa'b, I have a severe headache.'

'Shakun, give him some more balm,' Khanna Sahib told his wife.

'Hey, why don't you take the Sa'b to Afrabat? He's a big *seth*. He'll give you a handsome *bakshish*.'

Khanna Sahib turned to see who was speaking. It was the sledgewallah who had come unnoticed across the snow bridge and was now standing before him, the sledge resting over his shoulder.

'It's not a question of *bakshish*.' Hasandin said, 'I can't walk. I've a headache.'

The sledgewallah set his sledge on the ground. Taking the balm from Mrs Khanna he applied it to Hasandin's forehead. 'Now that you have brought them this far, you must also take them to Afrabat,' he said to Hasandin in Kashmiri and, picking up his sledge, made a move on.

Khanna Sahib resumed his journey. Usha and Jivanand had gone ahead. Khanna Sahib's son pulled at his hand, urging him to walk faster. Hasandin and the sledgewallah followed.

'Friend, why don't you fix the rate for me?' the sledgewallah said to Hasandin in a conspiratorial tone. 'I'll treat you to tea.'

'My head is bursting with pain. I'm in no mood to listen to you.'

'Take two tablets of Aspro with nice hot coffee. Your headache will disappear in a minute!'

'I can't afford coffee. I will feel lucky if I get salted tea.'

'I'll buy you a cup of coffee!' the sledgewallah said, thumping his chest.

A party of tourists was crossing the snow bridge behind. Hasandin cast a fleeting glance at them and then, catching up with Khanna Sahib, said, 'Sa'b, we can't reach Afrabat before one. You have to eat lunch and also catch the bus back from Tangmarg. If you walk down it will take you at least an hour to reach Donala. The sledge can carry you there in five minutes.'

'But I am not prepared to spend four rupees on a sledge.'

'How much can you pay?'

Khanna Sahib made some quick calculations. He had bought return tickets. If he missed the bus, it would mean a clear loss of eight rupees. Alternatively, why not spend the same amount on sledges and have the thrill of coasting down the snowy slopes. 'At the most two and a half rupees,' he said.

'I doubt if he would agree for two and a half rupees,' Hasandin said.

'There's no harm in trying. His loss will be your gain. See if you can fix up with him at two and a half. I'm not inclined to pay more.'

When Hasandin came back and told Khanna Sahib that he had been able to prevail upon the sledgewallah, Khanna Sahib regretted not having asked Hasandin to settle on two rupees per head. He turned around, 'Of course, I'll pay one and a quarter for the child. Even the buses charge half fare for the children.'

The son had gone ahead with his mother leaving Khanna Sahib far behind. Even Usha and Jivanand, straggling behind talking in whispers, had overtaken Khanna Sahib. The climb was so stiff that he had to stop at every turn to catch his breath.

'Sa'b, I've only two sledges,' the sledgewallah said. 'I'll get hold of another man. You can settle with him.'

'That's none of my business,' Khanna Sahib said brusquely. 'I'll pay one and a quarter for the child. It's for you to call another man and settle it amongst yourselves.'

Khanna Sahib increased his pace, but by the time he reached

the next turn he had started panting. In the effort, though, he had forged ahead of Usha and Jivanand.

'Your child is very smart,' an elderly man coming from Donala said to Khanna Sahib when he came panting up. 'He has already made friends with me and told me the names of all his teachers and companions at the convent school.'

'I'm not in favour of sending him to a convent,' Khanna Sahib said, 'but my elder brother has no child of his own, so he regards Kukku as his son and meets all his expenses.'

'You've done well by putting him in the convent. He's indeed a smart kid.'

'I was reluctant to bring him here. I feared the climb would be too much for him. But see how briskly he walks! I'm tired, but he isn't.'

The climb had become steep and the elderly man was having difficulty in breathing. 'Uncle, I'll help you,' Kukku said. And, holding the man's hand, he helped him to climb up through a short cut. In a moment they had passed the others and were walking along, talking and laughing, like one child with another.

Khanna Sahib sat down on a rock to rest for a while. He saw Usha sitting on a rock about three turnings below. Jivanand was sitting by her side, his left arm around her waist, talking to her animatedly. They seemed in no hurry to resume their journey. It looked like they would keep sitting there till eternity.

For an instant Khanna Sahib felt jealous of Jiavanand. Usha's uncle had put her under Khanna Sahib's care. His first impulse was to go back and criticize Jivanand for being fresh with Usha. Then he thought that perhaps it was a calculated move on Uppal Sahib's part to send Usha with Jivanand so as to entice the young man for his niece's hand. He knew no young man in Delhi would fall for a fat lump of flesh like Usha. Khanna Sahib's sense of duty ebbed away as swiftly as it had rushed up, and a long sigh escaped his lips. It was these people who were having the real fun, making the best of their sojourn, whereas he had got nothing out of it. There and then he decided to hire a sledge for the trip down, even if it meant spending a little more money. A sledge ride! It would keep the memory of Kashmir alive forever. In his imagination, he whizzed along on his sledge, tearing down through the snow.

The sledgewallah appeared from somewhere to the right, along with an old man, and stood before Khanna Sahib. Hasandin was also with them. 'Sa'b, this old man wouldn't agree to even two and a half rupees!'

Although only a moment ago Khanna Sahib had decided he wouldn't mind spending a little more money on the sledges, he could not bring himself to agree now that he was confronted with the situation. 'Never mind,' he said abruptly getting up. 'We're in no hurry. We can just as well walk.' Pressing his thigh with his right hand, he moved on.

The sledgewallahs followed at a distance, talking animatedly among themselves. Then the first one strode briskly up and said, 'Sa'b, the other man has agreed to charge two and a half rupees. He won't accept anything less.'

'One and a quarter. Not a *cowrie* more!' Khanna Sahib replied without stopping. Then he called Hasandin over and said almost in a whisper. 'See if he agrees to one and a half. It's my last offer.'

They had almost reached Afrabat when the deal was finally sealed at seven rupees for all the passengers, leaving the sledgewallahs to distribute the money among themselves as they liked.

SIXTEEN

The shoulder of Afrabat was an undulating patch of grass beyond which an ocean of snow stretched upto the peak. Standing on the grass, one could not tell what lay on the other side of the peak. Those who had come early were resting on the grass, reclining on their elbows. Others, standing on the edge of that patch were looking down below at the valley of Kashmir. Khanna Sahib's son was busy with the elderly man, plying him with questions about the peak and the range of mountains which stretched before him. Mrs Khanna, tired, had laid down to rest. Suddenly Khanna Sahib saw his sledgewallah walking swiftly up the vast snowy slope towards the peak.

It was an engaging sight—a black, ant-like dot crawling against a vast expanse of white. Leaving the bag with Khanna Sahib, Hasandin had spread out his blanket and was about to lie down when Khanna Sahib walked upto him.

'Where's that man going?' he asked Hasandin.

'He's gone in search of Mundi weeds.'

'Mundi weeds? What are Mundi weeds?'

'A medicinal plant. It fetches lots of money.'

For some time Khanna Sahib stood watching the man. Then he turned back and went over to where his son and the elderly man were standing. It was the same view which they had seen from Khilanmarg, but wider in its sweep and more magnificent. Mist was rising from the place where Wular Lake and the peaks of Harmukh and Nanga Parvat lay hidden behind the clouds. 'When the sky is clear one can even see the Shalimar and Nishat Gardens through powerful binoculars,' someone said.

'Which is more beautiful—Switzerland or Kashmir?' an Indian asked his companion, a European tourist.

'Switzerland is somewhat smaller.' the European replied. 'It could be tucked away in one part of Kashmir. But it's more developed.' He spoke with a typical European accent, softening his t-s and d-s.

It was going on to one when they sat down for lunch. Clouds were sailing over their heads. Through his son, Khanna Sahib had become friendly with the elderly man and his party. He offered them a *paratha* each, and in return helped himself to a veritable feast. The elderly man and his party also had a bottle of lemon squash, and fresh water in thermos flasks.

Guided by Hasandin, Khanna Sahib and his wife went over to where the sledgewallahs were standing. At the edge of the grassy patch a thin trickle of water was dripping from a mass of snow which had turned to thick ice. Khanna Sahib and his wife drank a few drops of water, but it did not quench their thirst. The water was icy cold, difficult to swallow.

Some youthful men among the party had cameras with them and were taking photographs. Khanna Sahib joined them and had his picture taken. He thought it a waste of film to use his own camera. These men were from Delhi. He noted down their addresses so that he could obtain prints from them even if they forgot to deliver them to him.

It was nearing two when some visitors decided to visit Alpatthar and the frozen lake. Most of the visitors wanted to turn back from Afrabat, but one young trader from Amritsar was averse to this idea. Now that they had come this far, why shouldn't they get full value for their money and also take in the frozen lake and Alpatthar? His logic appealed to Khanna Sahib. 'Have I spent all this money and undergone so much physical discomfort just to sit on this patch of green?' Khanna Sahib said to his wife. 'I could get the same view of the valley from Khilanmarg!'

When Khanna Sahib's son learned that his father intended to visit the frozen lake, he jumped with joy. 'Papoji, I'll also come with you!' he said. He ran upto his new uncle and insisted that he should also accompany them to the frozen lake. Although the man had decided to stay back and wait for his companions, he hadn't the heart to refuse the child and agreed to join him.

While Mrs Khanna was collecting her things Khanna Sahib went over to where Hasandin was lying asleep and shook him by the shoulder.

Hasandin removed the blanket from his face. His head was splitting with pain, his nose was running, and it looked as though he had fever. He rubbed his eyes and looked at the sky.

'Sa'b, it's getting late,' he said. 'You have to catch the evening bus. 'It's time we started.'

'No, no. Now that we have come so far we won't go back without visiting Alpatthar and the frozen lake. There's plenty of time. We'll go back in sledges.'

'Sa'b, you may go up. I'll wait for you at Donala.'

None of the others had a guide, though one of them had visited these places in his childhood. Khanna Sahib was not prepared to take any risk.

'You must come with us.' he said to Hasandin, looking very grim. 'You can't leave us like this.' Then he softened, 'Believe me. I'll give you a handsome *bakshish*. If you don't trust me, here, take a rupee in advance.' He put his hand in his pocket.

'No, Sa'b, that's not the point. I've a headache. I've caught a chill. I'm afraid I have fever.'

Khanna Sahib's child came running upto them. 'Hasandin, take me across that snow,' he said, pulling at Hasandin's hand.

For an instant, Hasandin stood looking at the spirited child. 'Child, I'm not well,' he said at last. 'You go with your papa and mama.'

The child curled up his lip tearfully. Hasandin was moved. He forgot his headache.

Just then Mrs Khanna took out the phial of balm and herself rubbed it on Hasandin's forehead, temples, and nostrils.

Hasandin took the canvas bag again from Khanna Sahib and led them forward.

They had gone only a few steps when they saw a stretch of snow before them. Crossing it, they reached a spot where the snow had started melting, but where they could not see the other side of the peak. Following Hasandin to the left, they saw another stretch of snow. In fact, it was the upper portion of the glacier which flowed down to Donala. Since the slope was manageable and Kukku had learned to walk on snow, he took a few steps on his own, but Khanna Sahib warned him to walk with Hasandin.

'Sa'b, the clouds have started gathering.' Hasandin repeated, 'It's likely to rain. We had better go down now.'

But now that they had come so far, not to reach Afrabat and see the view on the other side of the peak; not to visit Alpatthar and the frozen lake was unacceptable to Khanna Sahib. It sounded like a bad investment to him. If his wife or child had objected to going forward, or had they looked tired, he would have given some thought to Hasandin's suggestion. But the child was as active as before. Heedless that he might slip or fall, he had crossed over the last stretch of snow and was eager to negotiate the next crossing.

'Sa'b, we'll be late,' Hasandin said again. Khanna Sahib looked at his watch and then at the child, tugging at Hasandin's arm. He also saw the light shining in the mother's eyes, proud of her vivacious son. 'There's still an hour left,' he said. 'We can make it if we hurry. I must see the frozen lake. Then we'll go back in the sledges.'

Hasandin proceeded, holding the child by the hand. Camera and raincoat slung over his shoulder, Khanna Sahib and his wife walked along in the footprints left in the snow by Hasandin and the child.

When Hasandin had seen the child safely through to the other end, he came back to help Khanna Sahib and his wife, who were only half way across to the other end. The others stumbling along were left far behind.

Crossing the snow they were right at Afrabat. Khanna Sahib stood there, as if spellbound. The view at the other side was gorgeous. The whole place, under a cover of snow, was shaped like a beaker. To the right, far below, where the slope dipped away from Afrabat, one could see blue waters tinged with green churning up foam. Beyond the water was a deodar forest over which the sky was swiftly turning to a deep blue. Every now and then lightning flashed across it.

Hasandin was oblivious to the beauty of the view around him.

His headache had worsened and he was anxious to finish his job, go home, cover his face with a blanket and fall asleep. 'Sa'b, it's going to rain. There may even be a hailstorm,' he emphasized the words as if they had a magical power to accelerate his customer's pace. He wrapped the blanket tightly around his head and loudly blew his nose on the snow.

'If it's going to rain, it doesn't matter much whether we turn back or go forward. We'll be caught in the rain either way.' Khanna Sahib said. 'Let's go forward!'

He put on his raincoat and took in the valley and the snow capped peak of Kantarnag in one sweeping gaze. Silhouetted against the blue sky, the peak looked magnificent. But Khanna Sahib had no time to linger over the view. 'Where is Alpatthar?' he asked impatiently.

Hasandin pointed ahead. 'Just in front of you, over there,' he said.

Khanna Sahib gazed in the direction of Hasandin's finger to the right, where the snow had started melting and huge boulders of red stone lay scattered about.

'How far is the frozen lake from here?'

'About a mile, Sa'b.'

'Where can we have a good view of the lake?'

'From the edge of Alpatthar, where this peak ends.'

'Then let's go there.'

Supporting himself on his cane, Khanna Sahib proceeded towards the edge of Alpatthar. He had to cross the snow at two more places. He had just made the second crossing and was almost skipping over the stones when he was overtaken by a storm. Large hail stones came pelting down. The members of the other tourist party were nowhere to be seen.

Mrs Khanna, already wearing a raincoat, now opened her umbrella. The child covered his head with the hood of his mackintosh. Their progress was slow and halting. The clouds thundered and the hail stones became thicker. Khanna Sahib was in a state of frenzy and started running.

'*Huzoor*, let's go back,' Hasandin said. 'The frozen lake is visible from here. It's there, in front of you.'

On the far side of the mountain, the snow lay frozen in a perfect circle below them. Looking carefully one could see two or three such circles forming a bowl of snow circumscribed by mountains on three sides.

The storm had blown over towards Khilanmarg. Jumping over the stones and avoiding the jagged crevices, Khanna Sahib proceeded towards the edge of Alpatthar. In front of him rose another peak covered with snow, and down below, he could see a streak of green water resembling the stream of Verinag.

By now Hasandin had caught up with him. 'The snow will melt in about a month's time,' he explained. 'If you come here in August, you'll find it has become a regular lake. At present it's frozen. That's how it derives its name.'

Khanna Sahib turned round, called for his wife and the child, and then asked Hasandin to go back and bring them along.

Hasandin blew his nose and then tying the blanket round his head, went down to fetch them.

They took a quick glance at the circles of snow and then turned back, Khanna Sahib in the lead.

On the way he met the elderly man and his party. Greeting the man perfunctorily, he rushed away, saying he had to catch the bus.

The sky had cleared. Suddenly it occurred to Khanna Sahib that it would be an excellent idea to take a photograph of his wife and son standing against the snow-covered peak of Afrabat. He asked for his canvas bag, and took out the camera-stand. Fixing it in the snow, he hurriedly took two pictures. He was just putting away the camera when his son, overjoyed at the prospect of a sledge ride, ran forward merrily and slipped on a stone. Leaving the camera, Khanna Sahib ran towards him. Asking Hasandin to bring his wife along, he picked up the boy and proceeded towards the sledges, which were waiting to take them on their downward journey.

SEVENTEEN

They were small sledges, big enough to carry only one passenger apart from the driver. The child was eager to go on the first one. Overindulgent now towards the child, Khanna Sahib let him have the first sledge.

'Put your arms around my waist,' the driver said, 'and stretch out your legs. Hold fast to my waist. That's important.'

Khanna Sahib repeated the instructions to Kukku. He did as he was told. The sledge sped away.

In the second sledge sat Mrs Khanna. Mr Khanna went in the last one.

Khanna Sahib turned to have a last look at the view. Hasandin had spread out the raincoat on the snow. Stretching out his legs, he dug in the heels and plunging the walking stick in the snow, held it firmly in his hands for steering. Silhouetted against the sky he was ready to descend the slope.

Khanna Sahib's gaze roved over Afrabat. Usha and Jivanand were standing on the snow, their hands around each other's waists, their hair flying in the air. He could not see more, as the sledge started to go down.

Hasandin too looked at Usha and Jivanand for an instant, and then, at Khanna Sahib. Giving his head a slight jerk, he started slipping downward.

The sledges sped down at terrific speed. The drivers, experts at their job, manipulated them with great dexterity, their heels making deep furrows in the snow. Suddenly Khanna Sahib thought of taking a photograph of the sledge ride. Instinctively, his hand went to his waist, where he kept his camera dangling. His heart missed a beat. The camera was not there. Then he remembered that he had given the camera to Hasandin to carry. 'Hasandin!' he shouted back, 'Are the camera and the stand with you?'

The camera was of course there, hanging across Hasandin's shoulder. But where was the stand? Hasandin felt his *firan* pocket. The stand was missing.

'Sa'b, in the hurry I'm afraid I forgot the stand up there!' he shouted back to Khanna Sahib.

Khanna Sahib asked the driver to stop. The sledge went some distance further and then stopped. Hasandin came abreast of Khanna Sahib and put the camera strap round Khanna Sahib's neck.

'Sa'b, it seems I've left the stand on top of that hill. I'll fetch it just now. You go ahead. I'll follow you by the short cut.' Lifting the raincoat from under him, he slung it across his shoulder, and digging his heels in the snow, started climbing back.

Mrs Khanna and the child had gone far ahead.

'I've to catch the afternoon bus,' Khanna Sahib said to the sledgewallah. 'Drive as fast as you can.'

'Then hold my waist firmly. And put your feet in my lap.'

The sledge went flying towards Donala.

EIGHTEEN

It was a laborious climb for Hasandin. His feet had become leaden and his head was bursting with pain. His eyes became misty. He wiped his nose first with his sleeves and then with the end of the blanket, all the time feeling in his *firan* pocket. But the stand was not a needle that would get lost in his pocket. Either he had left it somewhere on the hill or dropped it on the way.

The only thing he remembered was that coming back from Alpatthar, he had brought Khanna Sahib by the shorter route to the place where the sledgewallahs had been waiting for them. There, on the chest of that snow monster whose feet stretched right down to Khilanmarg, Khanna Sahib had asked for his camera to take a photograph or two. He was just putting away his camera when Kukku ran towards the sledges and slipped on the stone. Leaving the camera there Khanna Sahib had rushed to the child's rescue. Hasandin had also run after them, but Khanna Sahib had stopped him and told him to collect the camera and other things and come down with Mem Sahib. When he went over to Mem Sahib, he found that she had already folded the camera and the stand and she then gave them to him. Khanna Sahib was frantically shouting from below, asking them to hurry up. Picking up the bag, Hasandin had escorted Mrs Khanna down the slope.

Hasandin clearly remembered all these details. But what happened afterwards—of that he remembered nothing. He clearly remembered having been given the camera. When Khanna Sahib asked him if he had taken the camera he had shown it hanging from his shoulder. But what about the stand? Probably he had put it in the bag when tying it to the sledgewallah's waist.

Hasandin turned round. Khanna Sahib had already reached Donala. Two horses were standing by, ready to leave, but the third one had become restive and was giving Mamdoo a lot of trouble. Probably Mamdoo had unsaddled the horses because of the hailstorm and let them loose to graze. Or perhaps Mamdoo's horse had just broken loose. Khanna Sahib, as he walked along swaying his arms, looked liked an ant. Of course, Hasandin could not make out anything very clearly from where he was, but he guessed that it must be Khanna Sahib. It could also be that the horse was not Mamdoo's but his son Idu's. The rascal had no heart in his work. He swore at him under his breath.

He wished that he could grow wings and fly to the place where he thought he could have forgotten the camera in the bag. By now the horse had come under control and been saddled. As he watched, he saw Khanna Sahib mount the horse. And then a doubt assailed him. If the stand was not in the bag...? He thought it imperative to climb upto the peak again and have a look at the place where Khanna Sahib had taken photographs, just to make sure. He started walking swiftly, looking about him carefully and wiping his eyes and nose with his sleeve.

He searched the patch of snow from one end to the other, but the stand was nowhere to be seen. There were three marks in the snow where the stand had been set, but no stand. Standing on the peak, Hasandin swept his gaze over the entire slope. In that vast expanse of white there was not a single black spot. He looked further down. The valley of Khilanmarg and beyond it, that of Gulmarg, lay covered with hail, only tender blades of grass, freshly washed by rain peeked out here and there. The clouds had sailed away and gathered at the horizon. It was still drizzling over Wular Lake. The sheet of white hail interspersed with green looked pleasing against the blue sky. But Hasandin's anxious eyes were searching only for the camera-stand. Sweeping over the scene they again came to rest on the patch of snow where the stand should have been.

Once again he looked about helplessly. Then he dejectedly spread out the raincoat on the snow again, and went coasting down the slope. He had to reach the Tangmarg bus stand before the bus left.

While descending from Afrabat at break-neck speed, Hasandin's heel struck against a stone and was badly cut. He did not realize it in the snow, but his heel began to ache as he ran from Donala towards Khilanmarg. Ignoring the pain, he ran limping towards Khilanmarg, and then waded through the slush on to Gulmarg. If the stand were lost, the Sahib would not give him a cent, and the two days' wages for the three of them would be clean gone. But if the bus had not left by the time he reached there, he would fall at his feet and beg something for his labour. Even if there were nothing for himself, the money might be just sufficient to compensate him for the feed for his three horses. But if the bus had already left? The thought staggered him. He prayed to Bapam Rishi not only for the bus to be there, but also for the camera-stand to be recovered. He cursed himself for not having settled his account with Khanna Sahib from day to day instead of letting it accumulate, especially since he knew that the customer was stingy and could not be trusted. Cursing himself for his foolhardiness, his fate and for Khanna Sahib's impetuous hurry which had kept Hasandin breathless all the time, he limped upto Gulmarg Hotel.

'They must be in Tangmarg by now,' the bearer told him. 'You have lost Khanna Sahib's camera-stand. His raincoat and walking stick are also with you. The Sahib was terribly upset. Take a horse and dash after him. There's still time.'

Hasandin was coming out of the hotel gate when he met a syce returning from Tangmarg after leaving his customers at the bus stand. 'I met your Sa'b on his way down,' the syce said. 'He was terribly worried. Better hurry.'

'I've hurt my foot.'

'Take my horse and hurry. I'll charge you only a rupee.'

On other occasions Hasandin would have straightaway dismissed such an outlandish proposal. But now he had no choice. He took the horse's reins, and the next moment, he was galloping away towards Tangmarg.

On the way he had no thought but to tug at the reins and spur the horse to greater speed. Fortunately, it had not rained between Gulmarg and Tangmarg and the path was dry. He took it as a good omen and thanked the Pir for it. He had a hunch that all would still turn out well.

He saw from a distance that the government bus was still standing there. 'Ya Pir!' he shouted and dug his heels into the horse's side. In a few minutes he was at the bus stand.

Idu and Mamdoo were standing near Sardar Harnam Singh looking scared.

'Here, hold the horse,' Hasandin said to his son and ran towards the bus.

But he could not reach the bus. Harnam Singh collared him and gave him one slap and then another. 'You son of an owl, you son of a donkey! Where's the camera-stand? And where are the raincoat and the walking stick?'

'Right here, Sardarji.'

Harnam Singh took away the raincoat and the walking stick from Hasandin, handed them to the policemen standing by his side and asked him to deliver them immediately to Khanna Sahib.

'And the camera-stand?' Harnam Singh turned round and gave Hasandin another resounding slap.

'Sardarji…'

'Have you got it? Where's the stand? Do you know the stand is worth forty rupees? You *sala* how dare you harass the visitors?'

Hasandin swallowed hard and mumbled something.

'What are you staring at me for? Where's the stand?' Harnam Singh gave him a slap and then a blow.

Hasandin fell to the ground and he felt as if the blows and curses of Raina and Karim Khan had fused into Harnam Singh's blows and curses.

'Lock him up in the police station,' Harnam Singh said. 'Meanwhile, I'll record the passenger's statement.'

The engine of the bus was coughing and wheezing, anxious to start. Khanna Sahib was standing at the door watching Hasandin being beaten up.

'Just a minute,' he said to the driver and got down from the bus.

Sardar Harnam Singh was already coming towards him.

'Sardarji, don't beat the man,' Khanna Sahib said. 'Anyone can make a mistake. The stand must have fallen somewhere.'

Taking out of his pocket not thirty rupees or twenty-five but a mere fifteen, he placed them on Harnam Singh's palm. 'Give him these,' he said. 'Five rupees for each of them!' And he turned to go. Then he took out two one rupee notes. 'Give these also to Hasandin—his *bakshish*!'

Outshining *Hatim Tai* in generosity, Khanna Sahib got back into the running bus.

Harnam Singh stood stunned for an instant. Then he muttered. 'The fellow must have found the stand. He was just putting up a show!'

'Yes, Sardarji, the stand was in his bag,' a syce boy said. 'It was there all the time. I saw it myself when the Mem Sa'b was rummaging through the bag. She hid it quickly.'

But Sardar Harnam Singh did not allow the boy to say anything more. 'Run away,' he said, slapping the boy on the face, 'or you'll land youself in the lock-uptoo.'

The evening shadows had lengthened over Tangmarg. In the police lock-up Hasandin spread his blanket on the floor and prostrated himself before the Almighty, who had warned him plenty of times. It was his own foolishness to have ignored the warning. He begged God to forgive him for all his sins and save him from further calamity.

In another room of the police station Sardar Harnam Singh, Karim Khan and Raina were holding a special meeting. Out of seventeen rupees, they had already sent eight to the higher police officials and distributed the remaining nine among themselves. Then they summoned Hasandin's wife, Yasman, and explained to her that Hasandin could only be let off if she somehow managed to raise fifty rupees. The government had to take care of the tourists. If the tourists were harassed like this, they would stop coming to Kashmir and people in the valley would starve. A new camera-stand would in any case have to be bought and sent to the passenger.

....

The Life and Literature of
Upendra Nath Ashk

⊷▭◉ ◉▭⊷

Upendra Nath Ashk

b. 14 December 1910
d. 19 January 1996

Ashk was born in Jullunder, Punjab and graduated from D.A.V. College. He went to Lahore in 1931 to pursue a career in journalism after teaching for about six months in his old school. In 1934 he decided to study Law to enter the judicial services and even practised for a while. Finding it against his grain he gave up legal practise and joined the *Preetlari*, a literary journal, as the editor of its Hindi edition. In 1941 he joined All India Radio as a playwright. Three years later he joined *Fauji Akhbar* as the editor of its Hindi edition for a few months before going to Filmistan, a premier film production company of Bombay, in 1945 as story writer, scenarist and dialogue writer. Two years later he contracted tuberculosis and spent almost two years recuperating at the sanatarium in Panchgani in the Western Ghats. Recovering from his illness in 1948, he decided to move to Allahabad, which was regarded as the capital of the Hindi literary world. He made Allahabad his home, established a publishing house along with his third wife Kaushalya, and stayed there till the end devoting his time to free-lance writing.

Ashk had started out as a Punjabi poet, soon after switching over to Urdu and publishing poems and stories in daily newspapers and journals at a very early age. He published his first short story in 1927 and during a literary career spanning six decades produced a corpus of over a hundred books in all literary genres. He is the first Hindi playwright to be awarded the Sangeet Natak Akademi prize in 1965. He received the Soviet Land Literature Award in 1972 for his contribution to the field of letters. In 1996 he was awarded the Iqbal Samman for his contribution to Urdu literature.

The Life and Literature of Upendra Nath Ashk

Neelabh

Just a few days before his death in 1996, while he was battling for life with a broken pelvis, bed sores, chronic asthma, arthritis, failing kidneys, and was almost incoherent from the pain, Ashk was asked by a local journalist what he would do once he was out of the present illness. His cryptic answer was, 'write'. In fact, he once said that whenever he stopped writing he felt as if he wasn't living. Even during his last traumatic illness he would dictate to whosoever was at hand till his failing senses carried him away to another world.

Ashk was born in a lower middle class Brahmin family, the second among six brothers. There was no literary tradition in the family as such. On being asked once about the factors that inspired him to become a writer, Ashk replied, 'poor health, extreme sensitivity, and the brutally maleficent atmosphere of the house.' Ashk blamed his father for his weak health and terror-ridden childhood: 'He drank a lot, was extremely loud and boisterous, and would beat us mercilessly. When he came back from work, not only our house but the entire neighbourhood would be terrified.'

Although his father, Pandit Madhoram, was a station master in the railways, the family always teetered on the edge of penury because of his waywardness. Madhoram was given to excessive drinking and dissipation, and could be extremely cruel when drunk. 'My father had beaten me so mercilessly time after time,' Ashk reminisced once, 'that my health had been impaired forever after. The other boys in the neighbourhood were unruly, uncouth and tremendous bullies; it was impossible for me to take part in their games and pastime.' Yet, Ashk's father had some rare traits. He was extremely generous, gregarious, simple-hearted, outspoken, and a man of his words. Though he did not amount to much himself, he infused in Ashk a desire to excel in whatsoever work he undertook.

Ashk's mother was a semi-literate, god-fearing, pious woman totally devoted to her husband. She was the hub of the family and instilled in Ashk a deep sense of right and wrong and the capacity to shape his deeds according to his principles.

Ashk's environment along with the sharply conflicting natures of his parents provided the material for his vast portrayal of the Indian middle classes.

After graduating in 1931 Ashk married Sheela Devi, his first wife, and started his career as a school teacher. However, after six months, he had to move to Lahore and struggle in the pre-Partition metropolis to earn while continuing his studies in law. He continued to teach and also worked as a journalist in vernacular dailies and weeklies of Lahore, one of which was *Bande Mataram,* the Urdu daily run by late Lala Lajpat Rai. Ashk finished his L.L.B. in 1936 with distinction and was planning to enter the judiciary when his first wife died after a prolonged illness, leaving behind a son. Her tragic death shattered Ashk and had a lasting effect on him. He gave up law and recognized his destiny as an independent, full-time writer.

Ashk's first poem was published in 1926. Though his early writings appeared in his mother tongue Punjabi, he later switched over to Urdu, and by 1936 was regarded as one of leading Urdu writers of the time. His first collection of stories was published while he was still studying and, drawn towards the stories of this emerging author, Premchand wrote the preface to Ashk's second collection of short stories, which was published in 1933.

Between 1936 and 1937 a series of tragedies befell Ashk, starting with the death of his first wife. Ashk emerged after this period a changed man who had left his flimsy, idealistic Elysium. Instead of writing stories from imagination, Ashk decided to portray the life and sufferings of the masses around him.

It was at this juncture that Ashk's writing underwent a drastic change. Ashk had already written a short novel based on his experiences in Shimla, and had begun work on his first serious novel, *Sitaron ke Khel*, when he met another budding author, Professor Faiyaaz Mahmood, in a local bookshop. Mahmood said he wanted to write a novel which would steer clear of the usual ways in which novels were being written. It would have no predictable beginning or end and would flow along like the current of life. This conversation was to have a lasting impact on Ashk's life and literature. He wound up *Sitaron ke Khel*. The theme of *Sitaron ke Khel* was inspired by one of the Sanskrit poet Bhartrihari's couplets. Overall the content of the novel was romantic, yet, one can discern traces of realism creeping in midway through the novel.

Soon with his stories like 'Dachi', 'Kakran ka Teli', 'Khilaune', and 'Pinjra', Ashk shed his romanticism and came steadily nearer to realists like Premchand and Russian and French masters like Chekhov, Tolstoy, Balzac and Stendhal.

At this time Ashk came into contact with Urdu writers like Krishna Chandra and Rajendra Singh Bedi with whom he developed lasting friendship. His interactions with Hindi writers such as Udai Shanker Bhatt, Hari Krishna Premi, Chandra Gupta Vidyalankar and Makhanlal Chaturvedi urged him to begin writing in Hindi.

In 1939 Ashk went to Preetnagar (Amritsar) to assist Sardar Gurbaksh Singh in editing the Hindi edition of the *Preet Lari,* but left in 1941 when Krishna Chandra invited him to join All India Radio, Delhi as a playwright. While serving in All India Radio, Ashk met eminent writers and poets such as Manto, K.A. Abbas, Faiz, Miraji and Rashid who together with Krishna Chandra and Bedi were all either working in A.I.R. or were closely associated with it. This group of active writers had a lasting influence on Ashk. He now embarked on one of the most creative and prolific phases of his writing career during which he wrote numerous short stories, one-act plays, full length plays, and commenced work on his magnum opus, *Girti Deewarein.*

Girti Deewarein was the novel which

Ashk had planned to write after his conversation with Professor Mahmood. It was to occupy almost fifty years of his literary career. It was his most ambitious project. Ashk wished to portray in minute detail five crucial years in the life of the protagonist of the novel, Chetan, a young man not very unlike Ashk himself. While doing this, Ashk also wanted to paint a panoramic picture of the Indian lower middle class life. Drawing his characters from around him, Ashk traced the journey of his protagonist through the various vicissitudes of his life, and placed the story in a historical context by setting it between the years 1931 and 1936, which were crucial years in the history of pre-Partition India. Not only is the novel autobiographical, but it is also a record of pre-Partition Punjab and of its literary and journalistic milieu.

In 1945 Ashk was invited by Filmistan—a premier film company of Bombay—to join it in the capacity of a dialogue and story writer. In between leaving the Radio and joining the films Ashk edited the Hindi edition of the *Sanik Samachar* for six months. Ashk worked with Filmistan for two years in close association with Shashdhar Mukherji and director Nitin Bose. He wrote dialogues, stories and songs, and even acted in two films—*Mazdoor,* directed by Nitin Bose and *Aath Din,* directed by Ashok Kumar. His dialogues for *Mazdoor* were adjudged as the best dialogues for 1945 by the Film Critics Association.

While in Bombay Ashk also came in close touch with the I.P.T.A. and wrote one of his most important plays—*Toofan Se Pahle.* The play was produced on the stage by the renowned actor Balraj Sahni who also appeared in it as one of the leading characters. Based on the theme of Hindu-Muslim unity, the play was later banned by the British government.

In 1946 Ashk contracted tuberculosis. In early 1947 he had to be moved to the Bel Air Sanatorium in Panchgani where he stayed for almost two years fighting the disease. Though bedridden he continued his creative pursuits—at times dictating lengths of his long narrative poem *Bargad ki Beti* to his third wife whom he had married in 1941 after separating from his second wife. That very year the first volume of *Girti Deewarein* was published.

In early 1948 the Uttar Pradesh government gave Ashk, along with the poet Nirala, a stipend to help him in his illness. After recuperating Ashk decided to settle down in Allahabad, Uttar Pradesh. During his fifty-five-year stay in Allahabad, Ashk devoted all his time to free-lance writing, and emerged as an extremely controversial and eminent author.

Besides writing, Ashk waged long crusades to better the condition of writers in general, presenting memoranda to central and state ministers, writing to various civil servants, and generally making efforts to bring author-publisher relations on an even keel.

In 1953 Ashk wrote *Garm Raakh*, a novel set in pre-Partition Lahore depicting the various facets of life in the metropolis. It was the first novel in which the left leanings of Ashk began to show. Though not a member of the Communist Party, Ashk had been active in its cultural and literary wing, the Progressive Writers Association ever since he went to Bombay in 1944 and, was actively associated with the PWA conferences held in Allahabad in 1952 and 1957.

In 1954 Ashk wrote *Badi Badi Ankhen*, a lyrical novel portraying the love between a young widower and a teen-aged girl in a pastoral surrounding. The novel drew copiously from the years Ashk had spent in Preetnagar.

The following year Ashk travelled to Kashmir and his experiences there led him to write *Patthar Al-Patthar*. It was a short novel, but with a large canvas, portraying the life of a poor peasant Hasandin who doubles as a horsewallah during the tourist season. It won Ashk much acclaim.

Between the publication of *Girti Deewarein* in 1946 and its sequel *Shahar Mein Ghoomta Aina* in 1962, there came a gap of sixteen years during which Ashk was in search of an appropriate form to take the narrative forward. In those years Ashk tried his hand at various genres. Stories, plays, poems, travelogues and memoirs appeared at regular intervals till 1962 when he at last broke through the writers' block and once again took up the story from where he had left it at the end of *Girti Deewarein*.

Four volumes of *Girti Deewarein* appeared between 1962 and 1974—*Shahar Mein Ghoomta Aina, Ek Nanhi Kindeel, Bandho Na Nav is Thanv I* and *Bandho Na Nav Is Thanv II*.

Also around this time Ashk started to write his literary autobiography, *Chehre Anek*. Using the third person narrative form, Ashk recounted in his typical vitriolic style experiences from his literary career. Numerous well-known literary figures find mention in the narrative. It is full of hilarious episodes and replete with black humour. Five volumes of this literary autobiography of sorts appeared during the next decade while Ashk was preparing himself for the last two volumes of *Girti Deewarein*, namely *Palatati Dhara* and *Iti*

Niyati, both of which were destined to appear posthumously. Needless to say that every volume of *Chehre Anek* created furore in the literary circles, and Ashk was labelled 'the M.O. Mathai of Hindi'. It was obvious that he thrived on controversy.

Ashk had visited Lahore in 1980 to refresh his memories of it. He went there yet again in 1989, soon after completing the sixth volume of his lifelong endeavour, to search for some important material before beginning work on the final part of his magnum opus. It was a successful visit and he was felicitated by the Academy of Letters, Pakistan as well as the foremost literary society of the Urdu language and literature there, the Anjuman-e-Taraqqi-e-Urdu. After his return he began writing the last volume, *Iti Niyati*.

However, health started failing him. Suffering all along from chronic asthma, arthritis, an enlarged prostate and weak digestion, Ashk had stayed fit through regular exercise and a Spartan schedule. Yet, the ailments had taken their toll. Besides his last years were spent in struggling to keep his publishing house alive, saving the family from breaking up, and worrying about day to day expenses.

Only about a hundred odd pages of *Iti Niyati* remained to be written when he fell seriously ill. He had vowed time and again not to leave the world before completing the novel which had sharply divided literary critics all along the years, as volume after volume appeared, between those who claimed that it was a singular piece of fiction and those who criticized it in no uncertain terms. Ashk drew his strength from the responses of his readers and knew he was on the right track.

In a way he had come to equate the life of the novel with his own, extending both as he went forward, not realizing that the body has its own limitations. His last illness proved fateful. When he fell down and fractured his pelvis, all the ailments which he had kept at bay through active living reared their heads for a final assault. Finally on a cold January day soon after his 85th birthday, Ashk breathed his last.

Once during an interview Ashk had said that writers should not be observed from close quarters, and explained that readers form an unreal and exalted image of the author from afar, and when they encounter him in his own surroundings where he moves about and behaves as a normal person, they are shocked to discover that he may also have his faults, and at times these shortcomings may be much greater or worse than those of regular people like the readers themselves. So, he remarked, read the works of an author, but do not come close to him or you might be in for a shock. I, as his son, was aware of this truth much more than any other person.

Yet, despite his faults, his acrimonious no-holds-barred debates and outspoken utterances, Ashk commanded respect even from his bitterest critics, and was ever ready to help even his enemy in need. 'I am no genius,' he often said. 'Whatever I have achieved, I have achieved through sheer perseverance and hard work, and, because I have this undying urge to write.' And this came from a writer of over a hundred books in all genres of literature.